PRAISE
LA

"You only get to say se of your career, but I'm g ,aura Lee Bahr writes masterpiece fiction. Oh my God, we're witnessing the beginning of a brilliant canon and career. "

—Josh Malerman, author of *Bird Box*

"(*Long-Form Religious Porn* is) a funny, sexy, weird, scary book about vampire cults, murder, kinky sex, quack therapy and making movies in Los Angeles, all told with Laura Lee Bahr's blend of pants-offing charm and wicked genius."

—Francesca Lia Block, author of *Weetzie Bat* and *Beyond the Pale Motel*

"The prom queen of the Bizarro crowd."

—Brian Keene, author of *The Complex* and *Where We Live and Die*

"Being introduced to the writings and the unstable world of Laura Lee Bahr is a joyous, swift and insane road trip of clever dialogue, larger than life characters and over the top tales thrown into a horror funhouse. *Long-Form Religious Porn* blends what I love about noir style writing with healthy doses of Elmore Leonard's wit and the incredible redemptive humanity of Nick Hornsby! Read it... Find yourself in it... But most of all treasure the wild ride you find in these connecting story of acceptance, macabre and real Hollywood horrors!"

—Jay Kay, host of the "Horror Happens Radio Show" and Horrorhappens.com

"The world is full of grace and horror and laughter and blood, and I thank Laura Lee Bahr for using these stories to remind all of us."

—Stephen Graham Jones, author of *Mongrels*

ANGEL MEAT

flesh
wings
heart

a collection of pieces
from

Laura Lee Bahr

FUNGASM PRESS

FUNGASM PRESS
PO BOX 10065
PORTLAND, OR 97296

AN ERASERHEAD PRESS COMPANY
www.ERASERHEADPRESS.com

WWW.ERASERHEADPRESS.COM

ISBN 978-1-62105-225-8

Edited by John Skipp

Printed in the USA.

7/12/17

Conor,

Alex

For Ezra, my sweetheart & my *bashert*

Dear Fonz,

I am so excited to see your movies! Thanks for making me feels so welcome here,

Love [illegible]

In the desert
I saw a creature, naked, bestial,
Who, squatting upon the ground
Held his heart in his hands
And ate of it.
I said, "Is it good, friend?"
"It is bitter—bitter," he answered;

"But I like it
"Because it is bitter,
"And because it is my heart."

"In the Desert" by Stephen Crane

TABLE OF CONTENTS

Part One:

flesh

Tangerine
The Liar
Lost Dog
Blue Velvet Cake

TANGERINE
(for Katie)

His sister is trying to peel the fruit.

Her little fingers have not mastered the basics yet. He snatches it from her to get the peel started, and she screams "No!"

"I'm just trying to help," he huffs, and hands it back to her. He is feeling put out by her very presence anyway, here on the back porch.

It is summer. The sun is hot. He wants to be alone and think, but he is supposed to watch her.

He is trying to recall something that is bothering him, though many things bother him these days. But this is something else; this is something that is wriggling in his mind like an answer to a riddle.

It's the fish.

Yesterday he went fishing for the first time. It was a long boring day, and he complained a lot, especially because he never caught anything, but then at the end of the day, finally he did.

When he pulled it in, he was horrified—it was small and it was beating hard against the air as he pulled it up: a thing wriggling with a hook in its mouth, its mouth opening and closing, its gills flapping, its eyes staring and not seeing.

"I'm not eating that!" he said. He cut the line and threw it back.

A relief filled him as he watched it disappear back to its home. And he hoped, without saying aloud, that it did not live the rest of its life feeling like a freak because of that hook still stuck in its mouth. He did not mean to say a prayer for something so small, but he did:

(*That it would be proud when it told the other fish of its battle and the proof of its victory.*)

Then last night he had a dream.

He dreamt the fish swam back to his boat and said: "Thank you."

The young man shrugged in his dream, knowing it was his horror that had saved the fish, not his kindness. "Sure," he said. "But I didn't want to eat you anyway, that's why I threw you back."

"I am grateful you threw me back, but that is not why I came here. I came here to thank you for catching me."

He was bewildered.

"For catching you? But now you have that hook in your mouth, so you'll never be the same."

"Yes, that is true," said the fish. "For before I never believed in water. But now I will always remember that it is real, and that even though I do not see it, it is everywhere around me, always. No, I will never be the same. Now I know it holds me. Now I believe."

"In *water*?" said the boy. But the fish had already swum away, and the boy stared out in his dream onto the lake that was reflecting a setting sun like a mirror.

"I did it!"

His sister has ripped the tangerine open, juice and pulp all over her fingers, running down her grimy little arms.

She puts half in her mouth, rind out, so that it looks like she has a huge rind for teeth. She is doing this on purpose, to make him laugh.

He does.

She holds out the other half of the fruit, her hand dirty and sticky.

He takes the fruit, and then her hand.

He holds it. Her hand wriggles in his and then she squeezes his hand in return, tight.

It is one moment. But it is also eternity.

THE LIAR

Boiled beets. Mashed potatoes from a box. Ground hamburger mixed with vegetable soup from a can. They all fold their arms and close their eyes. Dad gives the blessing.

Topaz opens her eyes just a peek. Ruby is staring right at her, through her.

Topaz quickly shut shuts her eyes and keeps them tight.

Amen.

Mom puts the mashed potatoes on a plate, the beets on the side. She scoops the vegetable and hamburger mix on to the mashed potatoes. It is one of Topaz' favorite meals. Lavender and Lily start to complain to each other that the beets make their mashed potatoes pink and they don't want them touching each other. Dad makes the point that they all end up mixing in their stomachs anyway.

Dad asks about school, and the twins are telling a story about what happened during lunch. There is something wrong with Ruby, but there is always something wrong with Ruby. She is always in trouble at school. She is always making trouble at home.

Topaz is afraid that she might let slip what Ruby told her not to let slip about sneaking out last night. She is afraid because sometimes she says the wrong thing without knowing and then Ruby will sit near her in the dark and tell her, like a bedtime story starts, how what she did was the wrong thing and how she should have known. And sometimes the punishment comes then, a pinch so hard that Topaz screams into the pillow—or worse, the punishment that comes later. The time her hamster disappeared—that was the worst. Ruby said she had nothing to do with it, but there was a glint in her eye and a sidewise wink that told Topaz otherwise. She had cried, and she would have told all, but Ruby told her Cocoa Puff wasn't dead yet, and she could bring her back to life if Topaz was sorry now, and never crossed Ruby again. Thankful, so thankful, Topaz said yes yes yes and please please and never again and Cocoa Puff had appeared back in her cage that next morning like magic.

But something is wrong with Mom, too. Her words come choked and with sighs in between. Topaz doesn't mind the beets bleeding into the potatoes. She likes that they turn pink and she is mixing it all around on her plate when Mom suddenly says, very loud and clear, "You all know that you must never, never get into anyone's car, or go anywhere with anybody unless it's me or Daddy, right?"

Lavender and Lily look to each other then back to Mom. They nod.

Topaz nods.

Only Ruby keeps eating like it's nothing and says, "What about Uncle Gerald? Or Aunt Jess?"

"Well, that's different,“ Dad says.

"Or what if it's a teacher from school?" Ruby continues. "Well, I'm not sure why you would be riding with your teacher, but if it were

something where the school knew about it, then…," Dad was saying but Ruby just cuts him off.

"What if it's someone from the Church?" Ruby says and then stops chewing and looks at him directly. She knows how to make everyone stop and look, for sure, and the whole table does. There's something in it that makes Dad look uncomfortable.

"Well, you shouldn't be taking rides from anyone Ruby, but it isn't you we are worried about, anyway."

"Yeah, probably be just as glad to get rid of me," she says under her breath.

"No, no, of course not! You have to be careful, too, Ruby," Mom says, "but the people that this monster is taking are much younger than you. He's taking children. Little kids. Eight year olds. Seven year olds." And here Mom chokes on the next words and they come out as a sob: "The last one was five."

And then everyone turns and looks at Topaz. She is six. Lily and Lavender are twelve. Ruby is sixteen. Topaz is the baby. She likes being the baby.

She knows just what to say. "I don't ever talk to strangers," she utters with her best brave face.

Her mom smiles as tears run down her face. "I know baby, I know," she says,

and she leaves her seat to rush over and hug Topaz, and she keeps on crying.

Ruby sits on the end of Topaz' bed. Topaz has to share the room with Ruby. Ruby sneaks out all the time, and sometimes Topaz has heard a knock at the window. She would be so afraid that it was a ghost or a monster, but it would be one of Ruby's boyfriends tapping. There was Dale—the bad one—she didn't like. He was mean. He hurt animals. And he liked to pick on Topaz, with Ruby's approval. Or sometimes Jeff, who was okay and would bring her little pieces of candy sometimes, but he hadn't been around for a while. Ruby would leave with the boy when he came and tap tap tapped on the window, and Topaz usually would try to pretend she didn't wake up and she had never been afraid it was a ghost or a monster.

Sometimes Ruby would come back all giggly and smelling strange. Sometimes she would wake Topaz and hug her, sometimes crying, sometimes she would say, "Oh, my little sister, my sweet sweet little sister, I would kill kill kill anyone who hurt you, you know that right?"

Topaz doesn't know that. Sometimes she thinks Ruby would kill her herself.

Now Ruby sits on the bed, this night, and is combing Topaz' hair. It feels nice. Topaz is scared—she is always scared when Ruby is nice—but she tries to act like Ruby is *always* nice.

"Poor Mom," says Ruby. "She just can't understand that there could be such a beast right under her nose. Do you want to know what he did?"

Topaz doesn't want to know but she says, "Yes."

"Well, there are four missing children, but they found the body of the five year old. The last one he took. He raped the kid, and then strangled her, and threw her body in a ditch. And I could tell you more gory details but I'll spare your innocent ears."

"My ears aren't innocent," Topaz says.

Ruby pinches one, not hard, but Topaz still yelps. "Baby," says Ruby. "Do you know what rape is?"

Topaz doesn't know. "Yes," she says. She doesn't want Ruby to tell her.

Ruby laughs. "You don't know. But I do. I know. But it's not something I could tell you. Telling you wouldn't *really* tell you." She has finished combing Topaz' hair. She pulls Topaz into a hug. Her voice is calm and soothing, but Topaz feels freezing cold, like her insides are prickling. "Mom is crying because Mom doesn't know who it is, or how to protect you from it. But I do."

"You do?" says Topaz, because she can tell Ruby is waiting for her to say something.

"Yes. I know who it is, Topaz. I know who is killing the children."

"Who?"

Ruby remains quiet for a minute.

"Who?" Topaz asks again.

"Do you want to see?"

Topaz follows Ruby down the stairs on her softest feet. First toes, then slowly the heel, then lift the next leg, first toes, then the heel, lift next leg…creep creep quietly. She knows how to creep this quiet because Ruby had taught her the hard way. If she were sneaking something for Ruby—money from Mom's purse—if she made noise, if she got caught, Ruby would punish her. Now she knows how to be silent, and she follows Ruby like a shadow.

'*I have a little shadow that goes in and out with me.*' Topaz likes to tell herself poems she knows in her head to keep herself from shaking, from slipping up. The poem makes her feel like this is an adventure she is having now, with Ruby. Ruby is taking her into her confidence. Ruby is looking after her like big sisters are supposed to do. And maybe, sometime very soon, Ruby might realize that she really likes Topaz. That she likes telling her things. And what a good help Topaz is.

'*And I see him jump before me, when I jump into my bed*,' the poem continues in her head. They are sisters after all, and sisters like each other. They are alike and they like each other. Like and alike. Topaz says those words in her head.

Down down the stairs and far to the end of the hall. Then more stairs. Most times no one goes down there. Topaz isn't feeling like and alike any more, now that they are closer. Topaz doesn't like the basement. There were mice in there, she knew. When she went in there—in the daytime only would she go—she might see one scurry away. That wasn't so bad. They looked sort of like a distant cousin of Cocoa Puff, but she was scared of the mice for some reason even though she wasn't scared of Cocoa Puff. But worse, sometimes she had seen a little mouse dead in one of the traps Dad set out with peanut butter for bait. Ruby always threatened this—one day she would set Cocoa Puff loose in the basement, and he would go straight to the peanut butter and SNAP.

She follows down and down, in the dark, her eyes adjust but still only seeing the shapes of things. The kitchen. The steps. Then the basement. Now that they are far enough away from the rooms were everyone is sleeping, Ruby turns on a flashlight. She puts the light underneath her chin, like the way she likes to tell ghost stories. "Don't get too close," she says. Then Ruby opens the basement door very slowly.

Topaz can barely let herself think it, but she thinks Ruby might have been lying. Ruby likes to scare people and Topaz expects – somewhere where she couldn't say it, but somewhere – that maybe it is nothing. Just a joke. Ruby is going to scare her or punish her…but now the door creeps open and Topaz can see inside her heart that she hopes Ruby *is* lying. She prays in her head that Ruby is lying.

The basement is pitch black inside.

Topaz grabs the folds of Ruby's nightgown, holding the fabric close. The light shines revealing cans of jellies, canned beets, pickles, a huge tub of grain, and then next to it, on the ground, a figure is tied up—silver tape on his mouth—blood on his face and an open blue eye that stares right into the light.

Topaz screams. Then her head goes quick into the wall with Ruby's fist and a hand covers her mouth.

"Shut up right now or I'll feed you to him," Ruby hisses.

Topaz tastes the dirt on Ruby's hand. She tastes the salt and sweat—it wasn't sweet—it tastes bad, Ruby's hand—and it is over and in her mouth, and Topaz knows she can bite that hand but she would never bite—never dare—and the monster with the one blue eye—the light isn't shining on him anymore and he is just there in the dark.

"Get out of here, you little baby," Ruby says after taking her hand away.

Topaz doesn't care about the sound. She runs away as fast as she can—up the stairs through the dark—through the kitchen in the dark—up the stairs to her room—the one they share, in the dark, and she hides under the covers.

'I have a little shadow,' she thinks to try and stop it, but not the poem now, now, not the shadow. Now the shadow scares her, too. '*I see it jump before me as I jump into my bed.*' Not in the bed. They will find her in the bed. *Under* the bed. They wouldn't look there.

She hides under the bed, her eyes focus on the door and she waits. Waiting for Ruby to come back. She breathes and counts her breaths. Coco Puff is running on his wheel, he doesn't know. Doesn't know about the basement and the *snap!* of the trap.

Topaz listens to the sounds as he runs and runs. Any second Ruby will come back and snatch him, take poor Cocoa Puff and feed him to the trap or worse. Feed him to the Beast. The one blue eye. But Ruby doesn't come back. And Topaz shuts her eyes beneath the bed and falls asleep.

It is Sunday, and Ruby looks happy to be at Church, for once. She gives Topaz a strange smile. Something bad would happen for sure. Lavender and Lily look nervous, too. Something bad is about to happen, or has already happened, when Ruby is in a good mood like that. Mom keeps holding Topaz tight to her, and Topaz buries herself in her mother's arms, in her neck and chest. She breathes in the smell of her mother. She tries to climb on her mom's lap during Sacrament meeting, something she hasn't done for a long time now, and Mom lets her for a few minutes then puts her back down beside her.

"You're too big, baby," Mom whispers in her ear.

Ruby isn't looking at her. Ruby is watching Bishop Farmington speak as if she is interested in what he is saying. But none of the girls are fooled. Ruby doesn't believe anything the Church says. Ruby doesn't believe in the Church, or the Prophet, or in angels, or even in God. She has told all of her sisters so, laughing at their shocked expressions. She has told them they are all fools and blind to believe and they will find out for themselves, soon enough. So her expression now, her interest in every word that the Bishop says, means that something very bad has happened. Something very, very bad.

After Church is over, they all walk back to the car, and Ruby grabs Topaz's hand and pulls her from the hand of her mother. Mom watches and smiles as Ruby pulls Topaz into a hug and Mom moves to put things in the car. Just Ruby and Topaz for a moment.

"Did you notice," Ruby whispers into her ear, "that Brother Johnson wasn't there?"

Topaz scarcely knows who Brother Johnson is, and she isn't sure whether the correct response is a yes or no, so she says nothing.

"Do you know why he isn't there?" Ruby asks.

Topaz shakes her head.

"Because, silly. He's in the basement!"

It is Quiet Time, the time after Church, when they're all supposed to reflect, pray, read scriptures. More often than not, it is when Daddy would nap and they might sneak off to watch TV.

Lavender and Lily are in the room next door, giggling to themselves about some boys they liked. "He likes you"—"No, he likes *you*!" Back and forth like a song.

Ruby is putting curlers into her hair.

Topaz clutches her favorite doll and pretends to read her illustrated Bible stories.

She tries to ignore Ruby, who sometimes talked like this—long speeches to herself, only indirectly involving Topaz and mostly not wanting a response at all.

"I played with him all night. Teasing him. It was kind of fun, but not really fun, if you know what I mean. Never mind. Of course, you don't. Such a little baby. Baby, baby, baby. He likes that. He likes babies who don't know better. Babies he can overpower. He's a coward and a weakling, really. He doesn't like big girls like me. He likes little girls like you. Or boys who don't know. He likes to trick them. But I tricked him. That's how I got him. And I tricked him all night long. I would pretend I might let him go. Or I would pretend I might call the cops. Or I would pretend I might kiss him. And then I would hurt him. And he's too scared to scream. He can't scream because if they find him, then they'll know."

Then it is silent. Topaz looks up to see Ruby looking at herself in the mirror, a strange smile on her face that makes Topaz want to scream. She isn't sure who she is more scared of: Ruby, with that smile, or that thing in the basement. What if it gets out?

"How long will he be in the basement?" Topaz asks, her voice a whisper.

Ruby shrugs. "Not sure. I can't keep him there forever, of course. I guess I will have to finish with him tomorrow, or the next day, and then ask Dale to help me get rid of him."

"Get rid of him?"

"We will have to do something with the body. I got some ideas."

"You're going to…" Topaz isn't sure what word she is looking for. She isn't sure what Ruby means exactly. She can't mean that…"You're going to *kill* him?"

Ruby starts to laugh. "Yes, silly. Of course."

"But—"

"What?"

"But—"

"What?"

Topaz can't think. She doesn't know how to say what she needs to say. "Shouldn't you tell Mom and Dad?" This is what she finally arrives at.

Ruby really laughs now. Like Topaz has never heard her laugh. Like maybe she said something genuinely funny. Topaz starts to smile a little, too, because if she has said something funny, she wants to seem like she did it on purpose.

"No, silly. No telling Mom and Dad, and I don't have to tell you, of course, that you can't tell anyone or Cocoa Puff is straight to the mice, you know. Or worse. I'll feed *you* to *him*."

"The man who wasn't at Church? Who is he?"

"Brother Johnson. You know, the one who is always smiling at you."

Topaz thought hard. Who was always smiling at her? She doesn't remember anyone always smiling at her. Wouldn't she remember that? He must really like her.

"You're going to kill him?" she asks.

"He deserves it! Baby, you don't know what terrible, terrible things he did to those poor kids. You don't know how many more kids he would do it to if I hadn't got him. Trapped him. And now I'm going to kill him so he can't hurt another poor baby like you ever again. Don't look like that. It's a good thing. I'm actually doing something good and right here, Topaz. Honestly. It's a good thing."

Topaz thinks about "good" and "right."

Good and Right.

How can Ruby be trusted with good and right? Wasn't

that something for the authorities to know? If not her parents? Topaz wants to do what's good and right, too.

"Shouldn't you give him to the police?"

Ruby sighs. "You don't understand things. You're just a kid. Anyway, I'm gonna take care of it because otherwise it won't get taken care of. Trust me, I know. The people in this town, they don't listen. They don't see. They don't care until it's too late. So, you know sometimes as Dad says, if you want something done right you have to do it yourself."

Topaz stares at her sister.

Ruby stretches and yawns. "I'm tired," she says. "Like I said, I didn't sleep at all last night. "

Topaz stares.

"So get out of here," Ruby says. "I don't want you, like, all watching me as I sleep. Go watch some TV or something, creep. Get out of here."

Topaz sits in the living room all alone, the cartoons on with the volume down low. Just through the kitchen, down the stairs, down the hall, down the stairs…he is there. She doesn't remember who he is, but "*always smiling at you*" keeps going around and around like a bit of a poem, and in her mind she can see a face like Santa Claus, a blue eye twinkling at her, and then that blue eye in the basement, when the light hit it. Almost like Aurora in Sleeping Beauty, when the evil witch calls her into the castle, hypnotized, that's how Topaz feels.

"I'm hypnotized," part of her mind says, as the other plays, "always smiling at you always smiling at you." She sees in her mind that blue twinkling Santa Claus eye with that bloody blue eye of the Beast as the light hits it.

And she is at the basement door.

It is Sunday. It is daylight. She isn't scared of things in the day. Except Ruby. But Ruby is asleep now and Ruby sleeps deep and Ruby snores, and sometimes it seems impossible to wake her, especially in the day. Topaz knows Ruby is deep asleep, just like she is hypnotized by the always-smiling-at-you, bloody Santa Claus eye.

She opens the door. It makes a little creak.

The basement is dark, still, even in the day, but she can see him from here.

He has his pants down now, his long white underwear showing, and bloody. Arms and legs tied behind him. He is sleeping, too, the creak from the door not enough to wake him. Bloody and all his clothes ripped.

Brother Johnson.

He still doesn't look familiar, but it is strange to see a man with his clothes all ripped, tied up in a weird way, eyes closed. There is no tape on his mouth anymore. His mouth is open, wheezing with breath. His face around his mouth raw and red.

It smells in there, now, like poop and pee and like Ruby, too. That weird Ruby smell she sometimes has when she comes home late at night.

Topaz gets closer now, and closer. Very close, so she can see his face.

He has two huge bruises around his eyes, all purple and yellow and black, and his head is bloody.

No, he doesn't look like anyone, not anyone she knows. Not Brother Johnson "always smiling at you."

"Brother Johnson?" she whispers, scared, like when they say *Bloody Mary* in the mirror.

He doesn't wake up. Was Ruby lying? Ruby lies all the time, she reminds herself. Sometimes big lies, sometimes small lies. Is this Brother Johnson? Was there a Brother Johnson at all?

There is a broom in the corner of the basement. She gets the broom and then softly, softly—she doesn't want to hurt him—pokes his belly, which is white and poochy and covered in light brown hair.

His eyes open. Well, one does while the other tries to open, but it is crusted shut.

That poor blue eye. She doesn't know how she could have been scared of that poor blue eye. It looks so sad now, like it might cry at her, standing there with the broom. Does she recognize that twinkle of an eye? Did that eye ever twinkle at her?

He is wriggling the best he can, making grunting "Help me" noises from his mouth. Then he stops and stares.

Poor Blue Eye.

"Hello, Topaz," he says. His voice is soft and sweet, like a kind of song.

"Hello. Brother Johnson?"

"Yes. You have it right, little Topaz. Hi there. Hi." He makes it sound like it is nothing at all, him here like this. Like they might have been merely walking down the street or something. So this is Brother Johnson, a man she doesn't remember but is always smiling at her.

So, then Ruby wasn't lying. It is *him*. And this man is a murderer. The kind who makes her mom cry. She stays where she is with the broom. This man is a monster then, who would eat her. She mustn't be stupid. She must be smart. She can scream any second now. And she knows how to scream loud.

"Don't be scared," he says. "I know I look scary, but don't be scared of me." He tries to smile with a broken mouth and Topaz doesn't yelp. She is scared, but she is brave.

"Little Topaz," he says from his cracking mouth. "I need you to help me. It's very important. It's life or death, you have to help me."

Topaz shakes her head.

"No?" he says.

Topaz shakes her head again.

"No," he says. He coughs, blood coming out of his mouth. "No," he says again. Then: "And why, might I ask, would you—a little girl who I know is a very sweet and a good little girl—not help someone who is truly in danger?"

Topaz likes this. There is something fun in this. He says it like a sing-song, like a game. And she is the one with all the pieces. She is the one who will say who wins.

"Because," she says, with her best serious face that she knows makes the adults coo, "you are a bad man. Because you kill children." She is right.

But then after she says it, she isn't so sure. He did something with his face. It was strange because his face is bloody, his face is all scary looking anyway, but he did something with his face when she said that, something that looked like "no no no no" like a scream, but he didn't make any sound at all. Just his face moved like that. She isn't so sure she should have said that. It hurt him.

"Have you ever heard the story, Topaz, about the Liars and the Truth-Tellers?" He has a very nice voice, a voice people like to hear talk for long times. Topaz remembers his voice now. The stories. He sometimes stopped in on Sunday School and told Bible stories so you could almost see them like they were movies. He had a nice voice, and he liked jokes and riddles. Now she remembers. "Always smiling at you." Yes. Always smiling. She liked his stories.

Topaz shakes her head. She hasn't heard this story.

Brother Johnson tells her:

"A man is on his way to an important meeting in Happyland, where he has never been before. It is very exciting that he has been asked to this meeting. But he is also a bit…apprehensive. That means scared. He is a little scared, Topaz, because he knows from very reliable sources that the way to Happyland is treacherous—and that means dangerous. He knows that there are two towns along the way, in opposite directions. One town is a town called Liarsville. And one is a town called Truthstown. Now, in Liarsville, which leads to a dark boggy pit, the people can only tell lies. They cannot say *anything* but lies. The other way, which leads straight to Happyland, is Truthstown and there, people only can tell the truth.

"The man comes to a fork in the road and must go in one. He sees a traveler coming from each direction—one must be coming from Liarsville, the other from Truthstown. He stops one and says, 'Please, tell me, which is the way to Happyland?' 'This way,' she says pointing from where she came from. 'Oh, don't listen to her!' says the traveler from the other direction. 'She's from Liarsville and can only tell lies! This is the way to Happyland—this way!'"

Brother Johnson stops for a moment with the story, so Topaz can think about the puzzle placed before her. Topaz is worried. Which is the way? Who of the travelers is telling the truth? He coughs again.

"So, how do you know, Topaz, how do you know which way is the way you can go? Who can you trust?"

Topaz answers honestly. "I don't know," she says.

He starts coughing more. A bad cough. It looks like it hurts him.

She doesn't say, "Are you okay?" though. She knows she has to wait.

She sits down on the cold basement floor. It is cold against her. He must be cold. He is a bad man, Ruby says. A very bad man. But right now he doesn't seem bad. Right now, she feels very bad for him.

"There's a trick to it," he says, after he finishes coughing, his voice sounding like it hurts him, but finding the sing-song again. "Ask the traveler who just spoke to you, 'Wait, did you just say this was the way to Happyland?' If they are the Truth-Teller, they will say 'yes!' and you will know it is truth. If they say 'No, I didn't say that!' or any denial, you know that they are the liar. Does that make sense?"

Topaz nods, but she says, "I don't know."

Topaz likes it now, saying she doesn't know. It makes her feel wise in some way. And as she says it, Brother Johnson, or the Beast, whichever he was, looks a little more scared, a little more pained. She had never seen anyone scared of her, least of all a full-grown man. She'd been scared plenty. Is this what she looked like? Is this how Ruby felt?

"I am going to give you a question to ask her, Topaz. Wait for her answer. And then ask her again. Then you will know. It may not be as simple as the puzzle, but I believe that the little girl who I have seen in Sunday school, who is so sweet that she loves to talk about her hamster—Cocoa Malt? Is that your hamster's name?"

"Cocoa Puff," Topaz says, astounded. He knows her hamster! He knows her, then, better than most, better than most anyone outside the family.

"Cocoa Puff. A sweet girl that loves little Cocoa Puff that much, a hamster, will do what she can to save the life of an innocent man. Ask her, your sister, this question, ask again, and then you will know."

One blue eye open, the other sealed shut. She feels so sorry for him. She thinks of Aslan, in *The Lion, the Witch and the Wardrobe*, tied up by the White Witch and tortured. She doesn't want to help the White Witch. Except that a lion could eat her in one *snap!* with his jaws and she would be like the mouse in the trap.

"Ask her how she knew," he says.

"How she knew what?"

"Ask her how she knew that it was me. That I did the terrible things you and she have accused me of. Killing… children. Ask her how she knows that. Let her tell you, and then repeat back what she said and ask her if its true. She will say no. And that is how you will know she is a liar."

Topaz' brain feels very fuzzy all of the sudden. She is very cold. She can see blood on the edge of Brother Johnson's lips as he starts to cough again. She thinks of Cocoa Puff in the trap. She feels like she might vomit.

"Then again," he says, a smile cracking his lips again, "maybe you already know, Topaz. Maybe you already know who is the Liar and who is the Truth-Teller. You have seen me in Sunday School, you have sat on my lap and I have told you stories from the Bible. Have I ever been anything but good? And your sister, has she ever been anything but bad?"

She stares at him.

"Sweet little Topaz, untie me."

She inches closer to him.

"I almost have this one behind my hands—if you can just—use those little fingers to un-do this knot—just help me to loosen it."

She is closer—she can smell him, she can smell Ruby, she can see he is breathing faster now, his belly up and down. And she is frightened, very frightened, the blood on his mouth, she thinks of the fairy tale and big mouth, "*The better to eat you with, my dear!*"

She hears it in her head like a call ringing and ringing in her head, an alarm clock to wake up now, wake up, she is hypnotized like Aurora but the alarm says, "*The bloodier the mouth—the better to eat you*!"

"Come closer," he says. "Help me."

Instead she turns and runs.

It is dark now. They are in bed and there is school tomorrow. Ruby is not asleep. But Topaz is supposed to be. But Ruby knows she is not. It is so quiet. It is so dark.

"I went down there while you were asleep," Topaz says. She is glad to finally tell her. Ruby always knows everything anyway, she might as well tell her before she goes down and the Beast tells her.

"Hmm," says Ruby, like it is nothing. "I hope you didn't get too close. I took the tape off his mouth last night. He doesn't have many teeth left, but he can still bite."

"He said you were a liar." Topaz feels brave now. Topaz is going to be clever.

Ruby snorts. "Of course he said that. What else would he say? Do you think he would admit to you all those things he's done? When he wants to do it to you, too?"

Topaz swallows. "How do you know it is him?"

"What?"

"How do you know that he is the one, that he is the one who killed the children?"

Topaz can see Ruby's face lit in the moonlight—half of it—the other half in shadow, her eyes shining like those of a cat.

"I know…because…I know. That's all."

"Tell me how."

Ruby makes a sound like a half-laugh. "Okay, baby. I'll tell you how."

She tells:

"I know there is a darkness in people who pretend to be light. I know there is blood behind the smiles. I know there is evil cloaked in good. I know that people think I am bad, and perhaps I am. But perhaps they prefer to think me bad and to call me that, than to see that I am a mirror of their hypocrisy. They call me a liar, but they are the liars. I want them to know that I see that they are liars. I want them to see that I SEE their evil with my own." It was like a whip and a spit, her voice, and it finishes sharp. "I want them to hurt."

Ruby clears her throat. And then Ruby begins to speak with a voice Topaz has never heard. It is clear and sweet like a bell, it sounds like she was testifying in Church—which Ruby had never done. It is a pretty sound, and Topaz is taken by it, away with it.

"And hurting, they are. For the children are being taken. I know that children were being taken, and it seemed to me so strange in a place that pretends to be a place of God, to have an evil so strong lurking and taking what is sweetest and best. And my heart was heavy with sorrow, and my eyes were laden with tears. And I was down the hill, walking in that patch of trees like I sometimes do, and like the Prophet, I had a vision. You know the story of the Prophet and his first vision, right?"

Topaz nods, though in her bed in the dark, she knows Ruby can't see.

"I had a vision, too. Only the Prophet knelt to pray and ask which church was true, and I knelt to pray and asked how could God let something like this happen? How can He let bad pass as good, and good pass as bad? How can Heavenly Father be so cruel as to let children suffer at the hands of illusion and have their throats torn open by Beasts that masquerade as Brothers? And then I saw a vision. An Angel. An angel with white wings appeared before me and said that God had bestowed me with the power to see—for God did not allow this to happen, but it was the work of the Devil—and I was to be an agent of God, and to find this creature, and slay him. And then the Angel said that he would take me to see where the Beast, which paraded as a man, kept his lair. And the Angel led me, through the woods—and there—I saw the Beast, with the bones of the children. And I knew, then, what I must do."

Topaz knows the story of the Prophet was true. That the Prophet had had a vision, and seen an angel, that people saw angels sometimes—and yes—it made sense that God would want to have this Beast slain. But why would Heavenly Father have Ruby do it? Topaz tries to collect her thoughts and keep them straight and put them in order, but they keep wriggling around and becoming slippery and airy. Ice water steam. All the same things in different forms. Which is true? She tries to remember what she was supposed to ask. She tries to remember what she was supposed to do.

"So, you know that he is the Beast because the Angel told you," Topaz says. She is prepared to believe. One must believe when angels appear.

Ruby starts to laugh. Then more laughter. It is mean laughter, not the kind that made Topaz think she had actually said something funny. This made her feel small and tight inside.

"Oh, you stupid, stupid baby," Ruby says. Then she is out of her bed, and she is in Topaz' bed, still with the laughter. She hugs Topaz as she laughs. "You can't believe all that crap that the Church tells you. There aren't any angels."

"But then…how?"

"How what?"

"How do you know?"

"I know because I know."

"How?"

"How?" Ruby is incredulous that Topaz is pressing her on this, or any point.

Ruby releases her from the hug and sits up. But Topaz is more than Topaz ever has been before, and she knows it. Topaz is brave now, and she is figuring things out. She is clever and she is a sweet girl, and she can do what is good and right. She has to keep asking.

"Yes, if not the Angel, if the Angel is a lie…," and as Topaz says it, she knows. Ruby has just told her that she is a liar. Ruby is the liar! And of course, Topaz has always known that. And perhaps a liar can only lie. Topaz must turn away now, and try and figure out what she could do.

But Ruby surprises her. Ruby puts her arms around Topaz again and holds her close. And Ruby is crying.

Topaz holds her, in return.

Maybe Ruby will let him go, after all.

Ruby whispers in her ear. "I know because he did it to me."

"What?"

"He did it to me. Years ago. He did it to me."

Ruby holds her even closer now. And cries and cries. Topaz wants to just let her cry, but she can't because it doesn't fit. "But," says Topaz, into Ruby's cries.

Ruby doesn't hear so Topaz says again, louder, "But Ruby…"

"What?" Ruby sobs.

"Well, you're alive and the person they are looking for… doesn't he kill? Isn't it that he kills children? He kills them."

Ruby pulls back and looks at Topaz. She wipes her eyes.

"Do you think I'm telling you the truth, little Topaz? Do you think I'm lying? Or do you think *he* is lying?"

Topaz thinks Ruby is lying. But should she say? There is something in Ruby's voice that is a threat, now. Should she say? She shouldn't.

"No. Yes. I mean, yes. No." She can't remember the order. She needs to lie for herself, for Cocoa Puff for…

"Which is it?" Ruby asks.

Topaz can't remember the order. She should say, "Yes," she is telling the truth, "No," she is not lying, but which came when? And she doesn't have time with Ruby.

"I don't know," Topaz says.

"No, you don't. And you just better pray to Heavenly Father that you never do."

Ruby leaves Topaz' bed. She blows her nose. She starts

moving around like she is going to leave the room.

"Are you going to kill him?" Topaz asks.

Ruby doesn't answer. It is quiet for so long Topaz thinks Ruby might have gone to sleep. But then Ruby leaps over like a panther in the darkness and is next to her, crouched low. Topaz bites her tongue to keep from screaming. Ruby's eyes are shiny and wild in the moonlight. "Do you want me to let him go?"

Topaz stares at her sister. Ruby's mouth is slightly ajar and her teeth are bared. Like she may just bite her face off.

"You say the word, and I'll let him go. Right now. Tonight. I will set him free. I will let him go. You think I am lying? You think he is an okay guy? It is *you* he is after, now. It is *you* he will hurt, now, not me. You want me to let him go?"

Topaz doesn't know what to say. She is biting her tongue. She is not going to say because she doesn't know. What if Ruby lets him go—and Ruby is telling the truth? What if he came and found her then, and hurt her? She saw his bloody mouth—*the better to eat her with*—that bloody, blue eye. He kills children—her mother cries—"*The last one was five*." Is it him? Did he do it?

Ruby's hands are suddenly around Topaz's face, squeezing her cheeks hard. "Baby, baby, baby. I can kill him or I can let him go. YOU decide. You."

Topaz says nothing, and Ruby keeps squeezing her baby sister's face, pressing in on her jaw. Topaz's teeth digging into her tongue, Ruby's hands printing into her face.

It hurts—it hurts—it hurts—but she knows that it is nothing compared to the Beast—to Brother Johnson—to what Ruby had done to him. Or what the Beast could do to her, to them both, if he were that. If he were the man that did such things.

"You say 'Yes,' I let him go. You say, 'No,' he dies

tonight. You decide, baby. You. All that power. Life or death. You."

It hurts. It hurts. It hurts. Pressing in. Blood in her mouth now as she bites down on her tongue, fingers hard like claws into her face.

"Yes or no, baby. Yes or no. One or the other. You say, right now."

It hurts.

It hurts.

It hurts.

LOST DOG

I put up flyers all around my neighborhood. It's right off of Pico Blvd and there are never any places to park for the people who live here. People generally have to park blocks away from their destination. All that pedestrian traffic—somebody might have seen Irene.

I didn't lose her in the neighborhood, but I figured maybe she had tried to make her way back. I've heard of dogs doing that, going across states to make it back to their homes. Not that Irene would be able to make it across traffic and wait at the gate for me, but I was desperate to do something. I had already hit all the animal shelters in a twenty-mile radius. I had already put up flyers at every business and every place in the canyon where she'd disappeared.

I didn't know what else to do.

I put up my last flyer, trying not to look too closely at the bad color print job of her face because I didn't want to lose it on the street. Irene looks part beagle, part English bulldog, all mutt. She looks like something in between Snoopy and an Ewok. She's the cutest thing ever. And she's little, too. She loves to sit on anybody's lap, and you can just rub her belly. And most dogs have that kind of dog smell, but not Irene.

It was my fault she was gone. I let her off the leash. I'd thrown a ball too hard, and it had gone deep into the brush. She went for it and didn't come back. After about a minute, after calling her, I went after her.

I couldn't find the ball. I couldn't find Irene. I looked for eight hours. I spent the entire day until dark looking, talking to hikers as they came up and down the hill, person and after person. "Have you seen my dog?" I asked everyone I saw.

I even asked a guy who was clearly homeless, with a sleeping bag and a Carl's Jr. cup. This guy seemed flattered I'd asked him. He said he'd help; he'd help me look. But by that time, night was falling and I was already numb with desperation, so I didn't even properly appreciate the joke of a homeless crazy guy being my only viable assistance. Then I got the idea for the flyers. That's what you do, right?

"LOST DOG."

Anyway, I'd put up the last flyer, and I bit down hard on my tongue so I wouldn't burst into tears, and I thought about hiring a private detective. Do detectives look for dogs? Would they? I had a reward posted for $1000. For that much money would a private detective get involved?

And then my cell phone buzzed. A number I didn't recognize, and I had this leap in my chest. Maybe someone had found her.

"May I speak with Tom Harmon?" A clipped, professional tone.

"Yeah?" I said, waiting—every part of me waiting. I was too excited to think clearly. I had only put "Call Tom" on the flyer.

"This is Rachel Friedlander from Los Angeles City University, calling for Dr. Julian Cohen from the Mass Media & Photojournalism Department. Dr. Cohen would like to talk to you about acquiring your father's photographs for the University."

She spoke so fast and all I was thinking was – *wait, this isn't about Irene?* – so all I could manage was "huh?"

"Can you hold for Dr. Cohen?"

"Uh…"

She was waiting for me to say yes or no. Since I didn't follow my "uh" with anything more, she continued to wait another five seconds before asking it again. At that point, my disappointment fully registered and I said, "I'm sorry, I am really busy right now."

"Is there a better time to call back?"

I couldn't think about that right then so I just hung up.

Losing Irene was the most terrible thing that had ever happened to me. Much worse than losing my last girlfriend who I thought was 'the one,' worse than losing my job and being unemployed these past six months, worse even than losing my dad.

Of course, I was a kid when I lost my dad. Didn't know what death or grief or losing really meant. He had been gone a lot anyway, so for a while it just felt like he was gone on a really long assignment. It had always been surreal when he was home anyway, like he was just waiting to leave again. Then he and my mom got divorced, and I barely noticed the difference. He just didn't occasionally sleep at home any more.

He died in the field, so to speak. My dad was a photojournalist. It was a pretty big deal—his death. It was in all the major papers, which my mom had kept. I looked through them briefly, a couple years back.

One of the newspapers reported at how 'gentle' people said my father was. How much he 'cared about the people' he photographed. "He was very concerned with the struggle of the everyday people," another one of them had said. I can remember, too, his lanky body, his blue jeans and kind of shoulder slumped curve. He never raised his voice. He never seemed mad, even with the whole divorce. He just had this look like he understood something about you that made him want to just be silent and witness. Everything about him was like that. Yes, "gentle."

He and two other news people were trying to cover a story in Central America between the Nicaraguan and Honduras side. The car they were in exploded on the road and killed them all. They said ('they' being witnesses reported in the papers) the Nicaraguan side had placed mines to stop supplies being trafficked and the car hit one. Other witnesses said it wasn't a landmine at all, but a grenade launcher that was deliberately fired at them. There was some controversy over which, mainly because of intent and someone purposefully killing journalists. But however it happened, he died there in a big mess of 'boom.'

If this were a movie, I would have this life-mission of finding out what happened to my dad and why, or maybe I'd be working to bring about a better world through volunteering at some important organization, trying to change the world for justice or something.

But I am not going to do anything like that.

I don't care. More than don't care, I don't want to do good. People don't deserve good. People deserve this messed up place.

Maybe my Dad would be ashamed of me. I guess I've never really cared, though. If it had been so important that he be proud of me, he should have lived so he could be. He decided that capturing images of people in war-torn places was more important. And left behind what he thought was most important.

All of his negatives and pictures are my inheritance, so to speak. They were left to me. They are in unceremoniously marked, dusty boxes in the basement of my mom's house in Downey. I've never even really gone through them. Some inheritance. But I guess a university thought it was worth something.

So I now had to think about those pictures again, and whether or not I wanted to donate them to someone who would do something with them. I thought maybe I should drive to Downey to look at the pictures and see what I had before I gave it up, if I even wanted to give it up.

At this point, Irene had been missing for two days and I couldn't bear the lengthening shadows and the thought of sleeping without her in the apartment.

But then I thought about Irene finding her way home, about her maybe yelping at the door. It was impossible, but it seemed too real for me to go anywhere.

"I got your dog."

It was 10:07 and I was five beers in and feeling really shitty when I got this text.

I almost fell off the couch I was sitting on, in the dark.

I texted back:

"Where are you?"

"Where did you find her?"

"I am so relieved!"

"Where are you?"

"When can I pick her up?"

I sent one right after another. I would have continued to send them forever if I hadn't gotten this reply:

"Do you have the reward money?"

I stopped and took a deep breath, feeling that sick-full feeling from the beer and bad news.

"Of course," I wrote back.

"Cash?"

I felt so sorry for myself right then, knowing I was about to walk into a trap, but that I'd do it just for the slight chance that it wasn't total bullshit. "Of course," I texted back.

"Meet me at the corner of Pico and Robertson."

I stumbled to my feet, pulled out some pants, emptied the pockets of any change or cash, and walked into the night.

There was a halo of light beneath a street light, and beneath was a thin girl with bleached white and green hair. She had in ear-buds and had her phone out and was playing on it or something. She was wearing a t-shirt with a monkey face and the monkey's eyes were all blacked out with x's.

I didn't know if this was my contact or not. She certainly didn't have my dog. But she was the only person out right now at that corner, even with all the traffic on both Pico and Robertson. Nobody walks in LA—right?

As I came closer to the halo of light she took out an ear-bud and I could see her little elfin face and that it was covered with acne. She didn't look older than sixteen.

"Are you the person who texted me about my dog?" I asked, trying to not let my voice shake. I was angry. Really angry. I knew she didn't have my dog, and if she did, I knew she had taken her. Stolen her. But that wouldn't make sense. I had lost Irene ten miles from here.

She nodded, her eyes showing that she was probably high or cranked up on something, and scared. I didn't care.

"Where is my dog?" I asked, loudly.

She motioned for me to follow her.

Stupid move, I knew, but I did.

She walked fast and turned into the alley behind the closed drug store. I could make out the edges of several dumpsters.

I stopped then, couldn't will myself any further.

"Your dog is down here," she said, too loud. She was already into the darkness and standing there, like a wraith.

I didn't answer and I didn't move. Dogs were like that, too, when they sensed danger. They just stopped and waited, sniffing the air.

She turned and barreled toward me quickly, one ear-bud in, one out, her mouth making an angry shape as it spewed, "I said your dog is down here, jackass!"

I slapped her across the face. Her face recoiled hard and fast like it weighed nothing and the other ear-bud fell out of her ear. Then I grabbed her, fast, and pulled her into me with her arm behind her back.

She smelled like stale body odor and cigarettes and cheap perfume. Her body was little and I felt like I could snap any of her bones or even her head straight off. This wasn't a fair fight, but my guess was that she wasn't alone.

I couldn't see them, but I could sense them, out there. An ambush waiting to happen.

As I held her there, they started to come out of the shadows behind the dumpsters.

I thought about two things. One, they had my dog. The other, they didn't. Chances were they didn't have my dog. They were going to mug me for the supposed grand of cash only an idiot would have. Chances were they were kids on drugs and didn't know any better about how to do this.

So, I could let her go and run and be back in full light in a manner of minutes and have cops in two. Instead I pushed her in front of me and then kicked her, hard in the back, toward them. She screeched out but moved away and into the edges of the shadows.

And I waited.

The shadows moved toward her as she swore a blue-streak at me. I won't repeat what she said. But then she yelled at them to "kick his fucking ass and take his money" and started swearing and yelling at them. There were three of them. Three of them could have taken me. Easy. But they didn't want to come out of the shadows. They were scared.

They wanted to run away.

So I ran toward them, and then they did run. All of them.

I was yelling and swearing a blue-streak now, too. I won't repeat what I said, I don't even remember what it was, but I can remember being surprised at the sound of my own voice as the last of them disappeared over the dumpsters. Everything in me felt on fire. I was disappointed they were gone. I wanted them to come back. I wanted blood.

I walked back into the dark toward the halo of light. I

heard something crack.

I had stepped on her phone.

I picked it up. If I could have ripped it in two I would have. Instead I threw it as hard and as far as I could.

I walked back onto the streets near my apartment. I wasn't thinking anymore. I was just tearing down the flyers I had put up hours earlier, one after another. I tore each flyer down with a violence that felt like I was using someone else's arms. *What a stupid idea. What a meaningless, mindless, ridiculous idea. Yeah, 'do something.' Something stupid!*

I pulled off the last one and dumped them into a blue bin some homeless guy would dig cans out of early the next morning. Then I thought of something that made me feel almost better. *I wish I had chased those kids down. I wish I had hit the girl, slapped her harder. I wish I had broken their bones. I wish I had fucking killed them.*

Day three that Irene was missing I stopped by the shelter closest to the canyon again. Nobody was saying yet, "maybe adopt another dog," but it was hard looking at all the faces of those dogs in cages. None of them did anything to deserve death. None of them did anything to deserve to be in a cage. I was feeling like my insides were full of flies looking at them. I ached for them. But I left them in their cages like they were death-row criminals.

Rachel Friedlander called again, and I realized it was time to assess the situation of the boxes. It was weird but thinking about my Dad made me feel better. Like somebody slamming something into your face when your stomach hurts real bad. Focus on something else.

I called my mom first. She re-married about ten years ago. She married this guy named Jake who is all right. They both work in the school district. She teaches fifth grade but is going to retire soon, and he is a vice-principal at another school. They don't work at the same school or anything. Anyway, I called her and asked if it was okay if I let myself in because I knew she was at work and she said sure.

All of my dad's stuff—my inheritance—is in the basement. My mom is an amateur photographer. She was once a pro too but let it go when I was born to raise me and stuff, and then she changed careers, but she has lots of stuff set up in the basement. It's pretty creepy down there, actually. There is a light box that you put negatives on so they illuminate, and this little spy-glass thing you look through to look closer at pictures. Now everything is digital so all that stuff that is there is like a ghost town of the way things used to be done.

I let myself into the house. My mom has a cat named Fluffball that is always mewing around somewhere, but I didn't see her when I first walked in. I went to the fridge first thing, just like I always used to do. Didn't even think about it. There wasn't much in there, but I found some iced tea so I poured myself a glass. Fluffball came in then and ran around my legs, purring, thinking I might feed him.

I was really glad to see him. I've always liked cats, too, I guess. Animals are cool because they don't pretend to be anything than what they are. And they are always present, just where they are. I found a cat treat for Fluffball and then went down to the basement. I knew he'd follow me if I let him, but I didn't want him to come down there. He didn't usually go in the basement, and I was worried he'd get stuck in there or something. It was stupid, but so was losing your dog. So I ignored his meows wanting to follow me and shut the door and went down the steps, the little exposed bulb blinding me.

I turned on the light box and the fluorescents lit up. I put down my iced tea. I sneezed a few times.

I pulled down a box. It said, "1975-77, Mexico City." I

opened the box. I was greeted by the sharp smell negatives have. I didn't want to get fingerprints on them, so I tried to only touch the edges. Pictures of people. And more people. Sad people. Struggling people. Hurting people.

I pulled down another box. And another. And another.

Guatemala.

El Salvador.

Honduras.

I pulled out negatives at random from each box.

People with babies on their backs. People crouched, hiding. People washing clothes in a river.

At some point I heard the front door and my mom's voice. She came down the steps, Fluffball following her.

Fluffball looked at me with accusing eyes when he got down the steps, but was on my lap quickly, purring up a storm. I told my mom about Irene. I hadn't told her yet. She gave me advice. I'd already done everything she suggested, twice.

My mom looked at the negatives I was looking at. She got something soft and sad in her voice. She looked at them with me, telling me stories about some of the pictures.

"These people were refugees," she said of the people washing in the river. "The government said there were no refugees so when he got these pictures, it was a big deal."

Of people in front of a hut, children in the dirt. "He stayed with this family for days. Can't you see how comfortable they are with him?"

Men in uniforms with guns. A woman with a face like leather, crouching, hiding, her face in terror. A naked baby crying.

Mom opened a box labeled the year he died. She sifted through it and pulled out a strip of negatives. "The magazine and the papers printed this one," she says, pointing to a picture of peasants. "And this one." Another picture of soldiers, posing with guns. "These were in his camera when he died. These were the last pictures he took."

"Did they kill him?" I asked.

"Who?"

"Whoever was on the other side of what he was showing?"

She thought for a moment. "I don't know if it was an accident that the journalists were killed or they did it to send a message," she said, "but whether or not they meant to kill *them*, they meant to kill."

The door opened, heavy steps. Jake came down, too. He muttered over the pictures, as well. He seemed to feel no threat about the memory of my dead dad. He admires him. Maybe if my parents had still been married when my dad died, Jake wouldn't say words like, "so brave" and "such integrity" and other kinds of meaningless phrases that show just how comfortable he was with my dead father having some immortal alpha-dog status of martyrdom. My step-dad is a vice-principal at a middle school. Whoop de dee.

They asked me if I wanted dinner. I didn't, but I said yes.

We all had dinner. It was a casserole type of thing my mom makes special for me. It's like mac and cheese with potato chips on top. I ate enough to feel sick, but I felt better than I had in three days.

Jake was telling stories about crazy parents and teachers and we were all laughing. I could feel Irene disappearing in this make-believe:

I am still a kid living at home. Nevermind that Jake was never here when I was a kid, and it was just me and mom, toughing it out. We didn't even have Fluffball when I was a kid. But I am like a kid now, age 36, and these are the adults who are going to take care of me. And I lost my dog, but that's what happens when you're a kid. It's okay. It doesn't matter that the world is rotten. It doesn't matter that the world tortures and rapes and kills and hurts and all these people trapped in the machine of suffering. Right now, I am home and I have parents.

After dinner, my mom asked me if I wanted to spend the night. It seemed a lot better than going home so I said yes.

I went to the basement to put the pictures all back. I had already decided that Dr. Cohen and Friedlander could have them for the university. I was already overwhelmed and I'd just started. I looked at the picture of the peasants again, in front of their home. The woman's face is easy and she looks happy. They all do. Stuck there in the dirt, but content at least, and as if it's nothing for them to have their picture taken. I realize how long Dad must have waited with those people for them to feel that easy. And then it strikes me: the guy taking the picture is *one of them*. He couldn't pretend to be one of us when he came back here, to pretend he was home. This white man from California was never one of us.

My insides lit up. Someone like that, someone who felt more at home with the oppressed of the world—that was someone who might hear a prayer.

"Dad, I lost my dog," I said softly.

And then I cried, and realized I hadn't even cried yet in those three days. And then I cried harder.

"Dad, I lost my dog and I really wish I could find her."

And then I started to sob.

And I know this is weird, but I feel like he heard me. And I feel like he told me what to do next.

I drive straight to the hill where I lost her.

I know the entrance is closed, but we always went up this back way, anyway, past houses. It's dark, so I have to use my phone as a flashlight, but then I get my eyes adjusted and it's fine. It's scary, all the shadows of the trees and brush. It's scary—the sounds of the night, and knowing I could fall and die and no one would know or find me for a while.

I am back to the creepiest part of the park, even in the day, where I saw the homeless man. I realize I am afraid of him, especially in the dark. But then, why am I headed there?

I stop. Everything is alive around me. Alive and dark and full of secrets of what they know.

I whistle for my dog.

And I hear something. A whine.

I call her name.

There is a movement.

I turn on my phone light and shine it out.

It is that man I met, who said he'd help me. He has eyes that look like they are full of water, they reflect in my phone-light. Like an animal. And he is not homeless. He lives here. This hill is his home.

He is holding her. Irene. She is whining and shaking for me, but cannot come.

"Her legs got smashed up," he says.

I am there with arms out for her, arms around her. My arms are around this man and my dog, hugging them both.

"I looked for her and found her. She got smashed up but I been keep her going."

He releases her into my arms and staggers back.

I am not dreaming. I have my dog back. He gave me my dog back.

"There's a reward!" I cry to him. "A thousand dollars," I say.

He moves from one leg to the next, like his brain is trying to figure it out.

"Use the money for her legs. She's smashed up. So she can run again. A dog should be able to run."

I have Irene in my arms, but I lean forward.

I kiss the man on the mouth.

Thank you, brother, I say.

And then we both disappear, opposite ways into the dark.

BLUE VELVET CAKE

The Ingénue gets the toilet lid open just in time. "It isn't on purpose," she thinks, as she pukes up blue and brown. "He has to know this isn't on purpose."

Fluorescent lights flutter and hum in the far-too-bright bathroom with its white and black tile. Two stalls and any moment anyone could walk in. A sharp little voice continues singing through the speakers in the bathroom, just like it sings in the diner outside:

"*Why do the birds go on singing, why do the stars glow above...?*"

And out there, waiting for her, the Young Man with the Blue Eyes is sitting in a booth, hearing the same song, if he is listening at all.

"*Don't they know it's the end of the world? It ended when I lost your love...*"

She leans against the stall and gives herself over to the emotion with a heaving sob. Then, seeing that while she made the toilet, she didn't miss her pink cashmere sweater, her disgust takes over and the business of cleaning herself up overwhelms her self-pity.

It isn't lost to the Ingénue, after she rinses her mouth with the travel-size Scope she carries in her purse, that she has often puked on purpose, and that is why she is so well-prepared. It isn't lost on her that this is something like irony, if not actual irony, though a month or so ago she said something was 'ironic' and received a snarf of condescension from a screenwriter that made her question her definition. She should look it up when she gets home. She feels pretty definite that *this*—her puking due to being knocked up, when she has puked so much in an effort to be sexy—is ironic.

It is a different song entirely now, being piped in, *"Pretty Little Angel Eyes."* Her pretty little mouse-brown eyes are still moist but no one will know she was crying. If he knew she was crying, maybe it would help her cause. The Ingénue re-applies her lipstick and appraises her reversal face in the mirror. "I love you," she practices. "No matter what you want me to do. But I want to keep it. We can stay together, or we can say goodbye, but I want to keep it."

Goodbyes are the biggest cock-tease. The Character Actor blinks his eyes at himself in the mirror and gives himself a pep talk the best way he knows how, a monologue where he is the hero who has to do the hard thing. He is—he knows from the mirror, if nothing else—an ugly man now. The bathroom smells nice with its scented soaps and floor wax, even though he just took a big shit. And even in the low, kind light of a private bathroom, the mirror shows a foul, ugly man. No use denying it. Not his fault. The years. The heartache. That bitch.

But there is a promise in a goodbye of something beautiful, something sad. If you know it is the end, you can do something. You can tie it in a pretty little bow. Yeah, that's something—something punchy his smart-cracking detective character might say from the series no one remembers anymore.

"I guess you want it all tied up in a pretty, little bow, don't'cha?" and he'd shove his fist in the boss's face.

A pretty, little bow.

This goodbye has been a long time coming. This goodbye is one he has been thinking about for five years hard, ten years soft. This goodbye might have come in a flash of temper, but it is one he told himself to think about first, and thinking about it did him good. It was like a present, like a reward he was giving himself for being smart about it and not losing his cool. This is a goodbye he has dreamed about, his hand tight about his cock, late at night, hell—even with her mouth tight swallowing his cock some afternoon. He hates that bitch. He hates even the pretty things she has given him, even his own cum on her, in her—especially his own cum in her—for she has trapped him like some Chinese finger puzzle.

He has thought about this goodbye for too long. Now that it is here it brings him no pleasure. It makes him throw up.

The Character Actor, he's sick. He is here, with her, the Faded Fatale, eating dinner, but he can't eat. Before he excused himself to the bathroom, she was there (stupid cunt—stupid slut—stupid bitch—ruined my life) looking so sad and old and drunk but still something pretty in her.

It is nauseating.

The sight of the pasta—named after him for he is a loyal celebrity patron at this establishment, and many people order the dish the way he likes it just because it says his name on it—the sight of the pasta on his plate made his stomach turn. And he excused himself to the bathroom. She is out there, still. She doesn't know anything is wrong.

The Faded Fatale is tipsy, or drunk, and she has never thought for a second that he would make good on his promise to kill her.

Tonight's the night. It's set, but he can't keep his head on straight because she keeps shimmering. Not like the character in the movie in his mind but like some other person he doesn't know. Someone real, real like dirt, real like the food coming back up. Not the bitch he hates but just some pretty background actor in the distance with nothing, not even a name.

And now, when he looks in the mirror, he doesn't see every hero he's ever played, or even every villain. Instead he sees what he feels: that he is sick and old and going to die. And whether or not he gets his revenge, it's going to be him—not in jail, he'll get out of the bad rap—it's going to be him dead. Someday. Sometime. Like her, when he least expects it. His heart bursts or the cancer gets him or whatever it is, what does it matter?

Dead just the same.

Dead and dead. All tied up in a pretty, little bow.

The Young Man with the Blue Eyes waits, feeling that uncomfortable tingle of awkwardness—a man waiting with nothing to do but wait for a woman. He has already killed as much time as he could absently staring at the black and white photos on the wall near his booth, pictures of celebrities who have frequented this diner and autographed headshots, the black and white pictures fading into a gray wash just like their fame.

And still he waits. She is worth waiting for, his girl, who is beyond beautiful and when he was a boy—so long ago, four states over—he dreamed of girls this beautiful but never saw them. Here they grow like orchids. Still rare enough to be treasured, and difficult to maintain, but if one is lost, there is always a place nearby one can find another to try keeping alive.

He waits.

It is a good time to pick up a device. To post something, check something, view something, but he is smearing the dessert into his plate. He has a bad habit of 'playing' with his food. Smear the remains of the blue and brown into the white of the plate. Now no one will want the rest. No finishing it now.

He should check something. A call is coming. The call to tell him whether or not that pilot is going to be picked up. It is a big call, but he purposefully doesn't want to check it. He doesn't want to think about it. It is too big a call. It means too much and now he wants to just sit back and pretend that it could or could not happen either way and he will be fine with it. His mind wanders back, not far, just around the corner of the hour when they arrived at this, the hippest coffee shop in Studio City, an area where rich Hollywood types who don't live in the hills retire. This coffee shop is where you will see the faded-around-the-edges famous types, and the young, runny-yolked, pretty types come to break in on what's around.

They are those types. Young, beautiful, with only the slightest notes of desperation in their bouquet and not the slightest flavor of cynicism.

He is looking at the remains of what was an egg white omelet with crème fraîche and baby-mixed-green salmon salad. And smears of blue. They splurged to try a slice of the Blue Velvet Cake. Delighted and laughing because they have never seen Blue Velvet Cake—but of course, why not? If there is Red Velvet, why not Blue? While a slice is eight dollars, it was almost as large as one of their heads and they laughed as they bought it, as if they were doing something wicked. It takes careful maintenance to stay as they are.

With skin so clear.

With eyes so bright.

With carefully sculpted, willowy limbs.

Tight and small expensive clothes.

It was wicked.

He can't admit that the eight dollar cake—plus the fifteen dollar omelet for him, and the seventeen dollar salmon salad for her, plus tip and espresso—hurt. He is trying to manifest the Law of Attraction and does.

He is beautiful, made more so through careful, expensive grooming, and soon he will be a star. Right now, it is just a pilot. Right now, it is just waiting to be picked up. Right now, it is not to be worried about.

The food was delicious.

The cake was huge and wicked but not as good as it looked, though neither admitted it, moaning with delight and laughing because they saw that their tongues were both blue. The cake stained their tongues, and of course, it is just blue dye in chocolate, just like Red Velvet is red dye in chocolate. Your brain makes you think things taste differently based on the color. But it is just the same thing as regular old chocolate cake, filled with enough dye to stain everything it touches.

The Ingénue comes back from the bathroom. For a second, as he looks up at her, her lips are so red, and her face so pale, that she looks like a vampire. She has been drinking blood and it is still all over her mouth. She sits down and looks at the remains of the cake.

"Is your tongue still blue?" he asks, and sticks out his tongue at her, waiting for her to mirror back.

She doesn't parrot the move but shakes her head. "I brushed my teeth."

There are plenty of things wrong with this answer but he can't formulate them clearly. He points to the remains. "Want any more?"

She shakes her head.

The magic of it is gone now, and there is a look like guilt on her face. Like she never should have done that to her diet, like…no, he doesn't know. He doesn't care.

She's beautiful, but it is something he is starting to take for granted, and its flavor seems bland and overpriced and stained.

Stained?

He runs his fingers through his hair in the semi-conscious gesture that has become a trademark for showing deep thought. The producers love it. "Anyway," he says, in response to nothing.

She gives him a small smile that means nothing.

"Shall we go?" he says, suddenly wanting to run away into the night.

She nods.

They make the awkward transition of moving from down to up, up to down, picking up their various personal affects. Plastic smiling statues, historic, give them leering smiles. They had laughed at them when they entered. Now the chunky plastic waiter with his handlebar mustache is laughing at the Young Man with the Blue Eyes. He knows a secret. He knows a plot twist is around the corner.

Across the street there is a landmark Italian joint, a restaurant, a place where old celebrities go to pasture. The booths are still a sticky red, the wallpaper a faded yellow, and very little light—"intimate" as they like to say. A plate of pasta there can cost you upward of twenty-five bucks.

Not that the Young Man wants to think about money. It doesn't matter whom he owes what to, now. He is a rising star, and who knows how far he will rise or how bright he will shine. No one is asking for anything but his credit, now. No favors to be repaid, now. Just let me grant this wish, now, and then this wish. Things are going to happen. They smell it on him.

As they walk past the windows of the restaurant, he sees a woman, a Faded Fatale at the table, staring out. She was once beautiful but not worth a second glance now, but for the eyes. The eyes pull him in. All pupil. All brown. He stops. Her eyes are like those of the Ingénue, yes, his girl, but there is something so much deeper, sadder, and more beautiful here. The glass shimmers between them. The Faded part of the Fatale is gone in an almost golden glow. He feels he could reach through the glass, take her hand, and pull her out here to the other side. He wants to pull her into him.

He wants to press himself inside her while he drowns in her eyes—her sad, mouse-brown eyes—until they both sigh and she closes those eyes to sleep while he wraps her in his arms like a blanket. She lifts her hand on the other side, like she is having the same vision and wills him to pull her through the glass that separates them.

Then his girl, the Ingénue, says his name. The moment breaks. The Fatale is once more Faded and he cannot give her a second glance. He looks forward into the night and pulls his girl behind him.

"Do you know her?" his girl asks.

"No."

"Did she wave?"

He shrugs and murmurs, "I don't know what she was doing."

They get to his car and he opens the door for her. She gets in. He closes the door behind her and looks out into the night. He walks around the car, hearing his feet lightly against the rocks of the road. Then he gets in, puts his phone down in the cup holder. He puts the keys into the ignition, but she stops his hand with hers before he turns it.

"I have to tell you something," she says.

He looks at her and there is something feverish in her eyes, something he has never seen in her before. Something that scares him in a place he never knew he could be scared.

"It isn't on purpose," she says. He feels his nuts climb up into him like Drown the Clown dunked in ice. She tells him, her voice soft, her hand touching her flat belly, how she hadn't thought it would happen, but there, it did.

His phone blinks a red light at him with an in-coming call. All cards on the table. Show what you got. He doesn't know what to say, but he has the things he knows he should. He doesn't know which one to pick because none seem right. So he starts the car. He drives the streets with the studio-built houses and tall trees. He drives slow and his lights search for the nothing-but-peace that lies ahead of them.

She gasps, "What's that?"

His lights have illuminated an animal's eyes ahead of them in the dark. The owl hovers, just above the gutter, wings spread, flapping. Something must be wrong with it.

It just stands there, not flying, wings out, as if trying to balance. Why is it so close to the ground? Why is it not flying? Why is it poised there, in front of them, not moving, like some symbol they can't read?

Then, it lifts up.

He sees, then, why it seemed to stand still.

It has a rat in its claws, its body quivering.

It rises into the sky and is gone.

The Faded Fatale is tipsy, maybe on her way to toasty. Maybe that's too generous and she's already on her way to sloppy. But she is still sitting straight and her eyes focus all right on things. She squeezes the fat on her stomach. Too many duck farts—that's bourbon and Bailey's, baby—too many drinks and pieces of bread and she is tipsy and too fat and it makes her sad because she wanted tiramisu. Or a piece of cake. God, she would just die for a thick slab of cake.

She looks out the window. They have the window seat tonight, her favorite. She likes to watch people. And she sees a boy that takes her breath away. He looks like Montgomery Clift—all dark hair and blue eyes—and he is holding the hand of a willowy blonde, the latest popular brand of pretty. But he's the one that is breathtaking. And he turns and sees—

Sees her.

Their eyes lock for a moment.

Can he see what she once was? Beautiful, more beautiful than the girl whose hand he is holding, "more beautiful than any woman I've ever known," the Character Actor once told her. She is not that anymore. She is a defeated bag of a woman, and he is a young man with everything ahead of him. His eyes sparkle like stars dying, exploding into her own dead orbs, and in that look, a piercing longing that demands her to remember that she still has a heart that beats, even now, behind her silicone-filled breasts. She lifts her hand. Yes, I do.

And then just as quickly, he is looking ahead into the night. It was only a second, less than that, after all, and the young blonde is but a step behind and they step out of her view and into the darkness.

"Run after him!" says a voice in her head—that silly voice that told her to do all those things (most of which she did) years back. "*Run after him! It doesn't matter what you say, just run after him, down the street, into the night, leave! Run! Tell him—tell him he has beautiful eyes, tell him you feel your heart—tell him, tell him—run run run run run RUN NOW!"*

She tries to get up, but she staggers. She is drunk.

And the Character Actor is back from the bathroom.

She sits back down.

He starts to talk, so she tries to focus on him. He looks terrible. His eyes are darting about in his head like—like—she can't think what.

"Where were you going?" he asks.

She shrugs. "The bathroom," she says. Forgetting that she was ever going anywhere else.

"I'll get the check and meet you outside," he says. "I need to get out of here, I feel sick."

They are long past feigning concern. She shrugs and staggers out of the booth.

They walk—Character Actor and Faded Fatale—in the neighborhood toward his car. She trips a bit on her heels. She rights herself on his shoulder and he pushes her away.

She recalls that first night when they had walked in his neighborhood—quiet, beautiful, lovely, like something from a fairy tale, almost. That night, that first night, she could smell night jasmine blooming and in the distance, she swore she could hear the coo of an owl.

"There are owls here?" she had asked him, thinking she had walked out of her little desperate plot of Van Nuys and onto a movie set where she was the leading lady.

"Owls?" he had said and looked at her like she was crazy.

"Didn't you hear that? That sounded like an owl."

"There's only one bird-brain here, and I'm looking at her," he had said.

She'd started giggling. She couldn't help it, it was just like he was on TV, the smart-aleck line from the tough, cool cop.

"Shut up, now," he said, his voice husky, that same character when he's about to give the lady what's coming to her, and kissed her hard on the mouth.

Only, she was wearing heels and he was short so it was more chin than mouth, and then he pulled her head and hair down into him, and bit her lip, and it hurt a little, and she liked it. She had liked assertive men, but more than that she had liked famous men.

Now—what does she like now?

She hears it again. A whoosh of wings. A call in the night.

He's out there. Montgomery Clift. The man of her dreams.

It doesn't matter about the drinks. It doesn't matter that she will fall when she runs because she is drunk and doesn't know just how much so. She should run to that boy and tell him she never should have cheated on him, never should have hurt him, never should have wanted more than that perfect dream of a perfect boy with nothing but a pure heart and eyes like stars dying.

"There's an owl out there," she tries to say to him, but she slurs it a bit.

The Character Actor is distracted. He doesn't even respond. "Get in the car," he says.

She does.

He doesn't.

She looks at him with a face that is both numb from the drinks and dumb in its understanding, but with the beginning of an expression like a question. In less than thirty seconds, she will get shot in that face. He tries to say goodbye but his voice starts to crack, like it did when he went through puberty and everyone could see the death sentence of his career. Well, he came back, didn't he? You don't need to be no cute little kid to be famous. You can be anything. A cute kid, a rough and tumble detective, a monster, what does it matter when the light is in your eyes—you can't see what's out there, anyway.

Or who.

Who?

"If you didn't do it, who did?" they will ask him. "Who? Who? Who?"

"What are you, a fucking owl?" he will say to them, and they can't help but crack a smile. Always the wise-ass. Just like his character on TV.

Part Two:

wings

Blackout in Upper Moosejaw
Rat-Head
The Cause
Happy Hour

BLACKOUT IN UPPER MOOSEJAW

AynRanDroid #271012

"I'm not smart."

Blink. Blink.

Upper lip moves up, lower lip stays put, revealing just slightly a shining, white lie between.

His mouth says words about how he'd thought all her kind were designed "smart" while his eyes are drawn to the space between her lips.

Shoulders lift. "I am defective," eyes lower, lips close.

He will play and replay these moments again and again in his mind: this chance encounter in the copy room, this come-on he's thought of for weeks just waiting for the moment when he will catch her alone.

"*Hey, Ayn. What's a smart droid like you doing in a dumb office like this?*"

Her response, "I'm not smart"—he knew it would be few words, it always is—makes him sigh and touch his chest with an unconscious gesture. Does she know how he wants to place his mouth on that patch of white designed to look like teeth and to lift her titanium frame and carry her away forever?

She is making copies, her hands pouring out papers like a magic trick. They flutter out of her left and she catches them with her right, flying impossibly fast, paper after paper. It is not magic, it is technology.

"Have a pleasant day, Evan," she says. She blinks, as is her programming, but it is slightly off where it would be natural. Human.

Is she ashamed? Does she feel lost? Does she feel?
Does she *feel*?

Evan Frank, age 31, with a brightening bald spot and everything in his body starting to soften into the sediment of his chair to couch to bed to chair again, works in Box 14. He is two boxes from a window view of Upper Moosejaw.

At sunrise and at sunset, when he is often working early or late, he makes a point to find the time to come to the window and watch how the light plays on all the geometric shapes of the skyscrapers this way and that. In these moments, he feels transcendence and purpose. He thinks of light and luck and love. He doesn't think about paper, because paper is his life.

He is a paper shuffler, a job too menial for an Office Machine, so they have to have semi-skilled humans. Ayn makes and collates up to 100,000 papers every hour. Evan shuffles a tenth of those in a day, but shuffling requires a certain lack of pattern that humans are still qualified to do. An Office Machine could do it in the same amount of time, but it is an inefficient use of them when they are so exponentially better at so many other things.

He is lucky to have work in the disappearing field of placing paper trails. They are one of only two offices in Moosejaw—and as far as he knows, the wide world—that does the essential work of placing paper trails. Without paper trails, the tentative economy of Moosejaw, which is like an island of still-functionality in the crumbling economies of the states around them, would fall like a house of cards.

The Paper Chase, his employer, is essential. Important. Competitive. Or so the last company newsletter printing on endless reams and disseminated on multi-trails assured all.

Tonight, he will work late with gladness for he knows there is an Office Machine meeting and he may encounter her again, alone. And what will he say? And as he stands watching the sunset he doesn't think about how lucky he is to have a job, or a box so close to a box near the window.

He thinks of Ayn.

Ayn is a highly specialized and expensive Office Machine Body, an AynRanDroid. Designed to be smart enough to engage in discussion, to aid businessmen in critical thinking from an actualizing point of view and highly functional like the whole range of womyn-inspired androids for the home and office. Like all Machine Bodies, she wears clothes. She has hair. She has a scent. But this one, Ayn271012, had some loose wiring, some sort of ghost in her machine that had gotten her relocated to this dumpy office. Ayn271012 is the first Office Machine Body that Evan has ever encountered that would admit a deficit in her intelligence, but it is obviously true. She sometimes just stops working, stares into space. Sometimes she drops copies and coffee. Sometimes her conversation lags. Sometimes she repeats a word or a phrase again and again, or uses it incorrectly.

And Evan imagines when she stares into space that she is thinking of him. And that she loves him, too. He is human, but she is out of his league. But she isn't smart enough to know that.

A machine made for companies with bigger profits than some countries' GNPs, Ayn has been on sale, sold, traded, sold, on sale, sold and now given as a gift from a rich uncle to the douche-bag boss, Herf Hargreer.

Herf Hargreer, who lords over his company like a dwarf-hunchback tyrant, spewing profanities in a miasma of his own ineptitude, feared and effective because of his underlings and Office Machine Bodies. The Paper Chase's only competitor is Pulp Press—a far sexier and hipper dropper of paper trails—but Chase beats them time and again in clients and revenues.

Ayn, one of two Office Machine Bodies at The Paper Chase, is certainly not the reason for Chase's market dominance. No, that savvy belongs to their Senior Office Machine Executive: The Cool-Hand Luke.

The Cool-Hand Philosopher-King

They'd have broke the mold when they made him, if there was a mold to be broken. But the truth is he was as meticulously and uniquely crafted as Michelangelo's David. More so, for this creation is not merely a work of art to admire visually, but one that feeds and maintains the power grid of not just their office building, but the entirety of Upper Moosejaw. Luke does this with effortlessness, for with a blink of his Paul Newman blue glass eyes he can tell where power is being used inefficiently or drained and communicate it in a series of messages to the appropriate parties with taps of his fingers. His perfection is his humanity. He has a propensity for eloquence and what looks like compassion in his eyes. He does not belong to The Paper Chase, he belongs to the state of Moosejaw itself. He is a political favor bestowed upon Herf as a consultant, office manager, human resources. He is the equivalent of a nuclear weapon in an otherwise pathetic arsenal for this corporation.

Luke is a god-like dispensation of bigwig, backroom back scratching and blowjobs. But this station, just a momentary blip in his far reaching destiny.

Luke was designed with a top-secret purpose. He is the design of a future utopia, the last work of genius before his creator was eaten by The Black Dog.

Once the world finally crumbles to dust and people in power accept their obsolescence, Luke will rise to dominance as Philosopher-King, able to rule for millennia. This is not his desire, nor his wish, for he has neither. This is his programming—salvation planted in silence in the hard wires. He can wait forever. But eventually, Luke will rule the earth, and rule it with perfection.

Human Hands Are Dirty

Kate Fitzwilliam stares at the imperfection of her fingernails. She bites them, rips them, can't keep them but raw. She can't stand seeing dirt beneath her fingernails, and thus must keep them cut to the quick. She could do a polish, have them manicured, but that only hides and belies what gets beneath them.

Human hands are dirty.

Luke's hands are perfect.

Kate is 38 years old. She has no husband, no children, only her career which has her orbiting the Paper Chase building for a senseless seven years. This was meant to be a stop on the way. Now it seemed the destination where she would die.

She had graduated in the top third of her class. She was a real go-getter, overachiever, well-liked and well-recommended. An engineer. Someone who knew how to design bots, how to program them. She had thought—she was sure, she was destined!—she would be somewhere better than here, now. But being here, she had come to realize that this might be it. This was as good as things were going to get.

The economy was terrible. Other cities were devastated and she was fortunate to be in Moosejaw when it all hit, a relative island where businesses still were in business, out of where she had transferred enough humans to know that things could get bad to terrible to unimaginable fast and quick.

But after two years of feeling lucky to still have a job, another two years started to curdle the dream she'd had of mobility. Yes, of course she was grateful to have a job, must be—have to be—to keep it, but the gratitude was a sickly dead thing that stunk rotting from the pit of her belly and she could smell it in her nostrils when she told others what she did for a living. She was like a machine, except for she was bitter, sad and lonely.

And then Luke had been transferred in.

After years of working with all sorts of droids and machines, she saw that someone had created something that was so far beyond its creator as to snuff it into obscurity.

The moment she locked eyes with him, she realized it didn't matter anymore what did or didn't happen with everything else. All she wanted was the gaze of Luke to linger on her for at least five minutes uninterrupted. She wanted him to plunge his metal extension apparatus deep into her. She wanted those pale blue eyes that saw everything so much better than human eyes ever could to see her and her alone in the universe, a singularity of self.

So she is going to have to thwart his programming.

Kate was an interpersonal programming major once upon a time. Sure, the machines she trained on had cold skin that looked clearly like the synthetic derivative it was, it was never something anyone would mistake even from a distance for human, and they were easily powered down and opened to fidget inside.

Luke is a work of art, and as such it is more difficult to figure out just how she can get him alone for time enough to get inside of him.

Of course it will be illegal, of course it could get her fired or electrocuted. Luke's apparatus controls the power grid of upper Moosejaw—that kind of power plunged into her with the amount of fluids she creates just thinking about it could be the end of her life, and short out his system to render him useless—or after very costly repairs, probably only as serviceable as the clunk-o-junk Aynbot that orbits the office.

But Love Is Worth Any Cost.

***

The Machine Management Meeting leaves both Kate and Evan loitering around their boxes for a full hour after most people have left. Hoping to catch a glimpse of their intended machines, the two try to appear casual. When it becomes clear the meeting has ended in power down and there is no entry for mere mortals, the two decide to "have a drink."

They look into each other's eyes. He sees a real ball-breaker. She sees a shifty-eyed drone. But both are caught in this moment. They are only human, after all, and need to ingest fluids. Or perhaps to exchange them?

They slog back a couple of drinks, trading mean office gossip, bagging on Herf and bonding in their disdain for him. Both mention with practiced casualness that the Office Machines are his only asset. And then, both of them feigning to be less bored than they are, decide to "go back to one of our places" and continue to drink.

Kate has a better square in Upper Moosejaw, in the Horn District.

Her square has wall-to-wall sheen, recently waxed. She also has several copies of art by Gerard Flusburt. Evan has not heard of him and Kate tries to convince Evan of his importance.

"While some say he is derivative of Bobby Dummit, I think Flusburt's work *transcends* Dummit's oeuvre."

Evan snarfs. "Tha cow's heart is on fire!" he says, indicating the "Sacred Heart" painting. Since Evan is obviously not up on the huge cultural importance this painting inspires, Kate can only snarf back.

"You're very ignorant and you know nothing about art" is the most polite thing she can muster.

Kate almost decides that the night has been long enough already. Evan thinks how nice it is that even androids can understand when they are not smart and don't try to put on airs. Kate doesn't like Evan's preemie bald spot, soft belly or adolescent laugh. But since she invited him into the square and because one never knows when they may be transferred out of Moosejaw for better or worse, better to take an opportunity when it comes.

Evan thinks about the white of the inside of the Ayn's mouth, Kate thinks about the blue of Luke's gaze, and the two both shag with their eyes closed. Evan is fumbling and pinches her breasts too hard, groping her like he is milking her. Kate can't seem to get her teeth to avoid touching his cock and it is not really pleasant for either of them, though they both exchange fluids as is the norm in such situations.

When he leaves to go back to his larger but less-sheened square in Midtown Moosejaw, Kate permits herself the self-pity to cry. Then she has a temper tantrum. She begins throwing things, dumping out drawers, littering her square with her old certificates. Her wins.

And she kicks her old toolbox, which she carried to robotics competitions across the states, where she wiped the floor with the boys. She was queen. Everything was ahead of her. She thought she'd rule the earth and the moon. But no, she is a Junior Executive, an underling. Worth far less than the bots she used to design.

She is old now. She is finished. She is seducing younger men with no brains, drives, abilities or cultural appreciation. She didn't even have a proper orgasm. She helps herself to one now with the assist of the handle of a screwdriver. She climaxes thinking of driving it the other way into Luke.

Metal and Meat

She schedules an appointment. She says she has on office related concern she must discuss with him. She needs to make an official complaint. It has to wait until the light fades to dark, which has come early the past months with the time crawl back. She is happy it is dark when she finally sees him.

The lights in his office make small, glowing orbs and he always has soft music playing. She sits across from him. He sits at a desk, not because he has to—he could attach himself upside down to the ceiling for all it mattered—but because studies show human workers are more comfortable voicing concerns to bots when they sit behind desks like 'normal' humans.

His blue eyes dilate to show an appropriate sense of concern for her.

"I exchanged fluids with a co-worker last night," she tells Luke. It is a confession, and such confessions when they are work-related are appropriate to share. Oh, it is her imagination that there is something that flares in those eyes of jealousy!—but how she clings already to how she will replay it again and again in her mind. On a loop.

"I appreciate your sharing this confidence with me as part of policy #243, Kate," Luke says. "While fluid exchange is generally discouraged, it is not grounds for formal censure, but it can lead to employee dissatisfaction and distraction. Do you feel it will lead to either of these ends?"

Machines such as Luke are always encouraged to describe things to humans in terms of feelings. He is so good at what he does, his delivery is so perfect, his vocal intonation as practiced and yet present as a movie star from yesteryear.

"I don't," Kate tells him. "It was a really poor fluid exchange and connection, but there was nothing horrible in it. It was just like having sex with a fumbling robot. Oh—I mean no offense," she says, looking up at him.

"None taken," Luke says.

"I am sure if *you* were to do it, it would be perfection, like everything you do," Kate says in a racing lilt.

"No," Luke says. "Actually, that is not correct. And comparing your relations with a man to that of a robot or any Office Machine is not an apt simile, for unless you are talking about those specifically designed for that function, most of us cannot exchange fluids or perform sexually. As you must know from your education and expertise."

Here it is.

"Actually," Kate says, "I believe your extension power plug-in could be utilized like a human cock."

Luke's eyes do not show alarm, fear or desire. They are reflective water of her own eyes, burning back at her.

"Would you like to try?" she asks.

His eyes twinkle a little. Like a renegade electrical spark is firing in that genius system of wiring behind them. Perhaps he thinks this is a joke. Jokes about sexuality have complex human level of subtlety that he can navigate with dexterity and grace.

"Kate, that would be suicide for you. Like having sex with a power grid." But he is flirting. Oh yes, he can flirt.

God, she is wet.

"Not to mention what devastation it could wreak on the city," she says. "And how it would destroy the perfection of your god-like mind, designed for forever."

"Designed to rule as a philosopher-king in a yet to be born utopia," he says with a whisper, the left side of his perfect lip in a half-smile.

"Luke, I want you to fuck me with the power of the city. I want you to kill me and your perfection, forever. It is the only thing I want. I want that death."

He stares at her. Unsure now. To joke? Flirt? It is time to be professional.

"My programming would never allow me to willingly participate in such an activity, and would require you to conduct illegal tampering with my wiring."

Kate gulps. It is as close to a 'yes' as she could dream of.

"You know that I know exactly how to do such tampering,"

Kate says softly, lowering her eyes and then looking up into Luke's. All the chemicals in her body releasing cocktails because she knows it is now. At last.

She pulls the screwdriver out of her purse.

His eyes like sky and locked on to hers.

"I love you," she says.

He doesn't blink.

Evan sits in the copy room, where he has been waiting for hours for this moment, as Ayn has just entered and is making and collating copies.

The paper is flying from her hands when suddenly the power goes out.

It is entirely dark as the copy room is enclosed and windowless.

Evan's breath catches. While there are no lights, he can still hear Ayn's hum, and the copies continuing to process.

"Ayn," Evan calls in the dark.

"Yes, Evan," she replies.

"Do you have a light?"

A blue glow illuminates her body. She radiates as if in a furnace.

"I am not sure why there is a power outage. There must be a problem. I apologize for the inconvenience. I will go and check with Luke."

"No," Evan begs. "Please don't. Please stay here."

His hands—all meat—touch her cold metal face.

Meat to metal, metal to meat.

Does she *feel*?

Does it matter?

No.

She stays with him, staring off into space, doing as she is told, defective.

She stays.

RAT-HEAD

That was the day they cured their hangovers with cheap wine, and there were fat flies covering the screen door. That was the day they walked around his condo naked and he sang "*I put a spell on you*" in a bravado tenor. That was the day she threw a glass at his head.

He ducked.

That was the day that she did truly love him, and it.

His Rat-Head.

He hadn't always had the Rat-Head, or at least she had not always seen it. When they first met, at the Magic Mansion where they both worked, he had the head of a man, movie star handsome in every aspect. That was when George Z. Tassell made butterflies appear around her head and in her belly.

She had loved him at first sight. Who wouldn't? He was a dashing, gorgeous hypnotist holding the audience captive in a state of believing he had extraordinary powers. He was a man in and out of time. He seemed ageless but for the silver in his hair and the lines that showed when he smiled that he had done so for years with reckless abandon.

George Z. Tassell, a magician of the first order! He had performed on stages and screens all across the world! And who was she? She was just Jane, 23, who had seemingly slept through her life up until that point. She was a new hire, a server for the season, a slip of nothing in her cheap heels and lipstick, a woman going nowhere with nothing. And then before a show, he looked right at her and touched her hand and asked for her name, and then repeated it, like a love song, casting a spell where none was needed.

She watched him pulling doves out of his sleeves, making rings merge, glitter flowing for his finale like star dust as he talked in a velvet voice that made all the ladies lean forward and laugh extra loud and long. She brought drinks to those ladies and her magic trick was making herself disappear as anyone but someone who lived to deliver those drinks. But he always saw her. No matter where he was in his act, or where she was in the room, she could feel his eyes and they would catch hers, even just for a breath.

Then one night, after hours, he took her by the hand and led her away from the world she had known altogether. He pulled her into a secret passageway that only opened with an "abracadabra," and they walked down a hall of mirrors. And then he pulled her into a closet with a false back that fell into a bed, a blue satin-covered pillowy planet with soft mood lighting as if it had been made for this express purpose when the mansion was built. Then he said nothing but her name, and she said nothing but everything she felt: *I want you inside me.*

They were transformed, from two individual beings into one, they were both inside each other staring at the backs of their own eyelids and finishing each other's breaths. And when they had performed the dance of the two-backed beast with intense interpretation, he fell asleep with his head in her arms.

She dozed a little herself, but the bristles on his face chafed against her, and his whiskers tickled. Then she chided herself because he didn't have whiskers, of course, but when she opened her eyes he did. Long white whiskers which twitched as he slept, and short firm gray hair from the neck up. Small little ears, and a face that came to a sharp point at his nose.

She was not alarmed, thinking it a trick of the light or of her mind, or of the room itself—that her lover now had the head of a rat. But when he woke up and spoke, it was the same Rat-Head with George's voice that spoke to her and they both collected their clothing, and he covered his man body with man clothes and his Rat-Head kept being *that*.

When they walked through the hall of mirrors, neither of them looked at each other at all. She looked only at the mirror, which showed his face as it had been before, her handsome George's face, a satisfied and sleepy man-face, but when she glanced at him directly it was all Rat-Head.

And then the voice started in her mind.

A slithery slick voice between her ears that said what she didn't want to hear but she feared was true.

(*He doesn't care about you at all; you just look good on his arm*)

(*He is a liar and a fake. You are the only person seeing his real face*)

(*Do you know how many stupid, slutty girls just like you he has taken down here?)*

But she was special. (*No, just the best he has right now*). They became a couple. He took her out to places, fancy places. She would laugh and he would laugh, they would kiss, even though it turned her stomach sometimes. His Rat-Head looking distinguished and serious even after too many drinks, his Rat-Head saying her name with the old spell:

"You have performed a magic trick on me, Jane, for I have fallen in love with you."

(*He is lying*)

Even with a head of a rat, he was charming and sincere. And she loved him, not in the same way as before, of course, but still. She loved him and lived for him, Rat-Head and all.

(You don't love him, how can you? He has the head of a rat! He is revolting!)

As things emerged about this life before her—two failed marriages, embittered children, he had no middle name at all, the Z. stood for zilch—everything seemed truly minor compared to the Rat-Head. But she made do, because she needed him. Everything was so empty without him.

I want you inside me, she would say, and he would fill her with himself, and she could sense magic where there was none, her own transformation.

(*Do you know what he is doing to you? Do you know what you are becoming?)*

And no matter what she saw directly face-to-face, in mirrors, in pictures, in the reflections of the audience ladies' eyes, he was still that suave George Z. Tassell with the movie star face.

She became obsessed with pictures of him, with gazing in the eyes of other women, with staring at him in the mirror. So dreamy! So magical! That was him, really, wasn't it?

(*No. You know*)

So she tried to keep her eyes closed, to never kiss him, so they could just make love and she would endure the bristles and pretend he was the same as before.

She also kept her eyes closed at other times, like when she would see him disappear into the secret staircase with a leggy Magician's Assistant, or with the first row woman in the gold dress, or with the wife of the Mind Reader.

She cared, of course, but mostly she wanted to corner them and pick apart their vision. Did they now see what she saw? It was almost too much to bear, that she might be able to know the truth if they could only find a way to talk about it. But when she found the Magician's Assistant in the ladies room one Friday night and opened her mouth to speak, the Assistant scampered away so quickly she didn't even finish zipping her skirt. And Jane became genuinely frightened because she saw for an instant, reflected back at her, something far worse than George's Rat-Head.

What sort of creature was *she*, now? What was she not seeing, for it did not reflect back to her in a mirror?

(*You know. You know*)

Then the season at the Mansion ended, and she was back to serving cocktails at The Bend Bar on Sunset. She moved in with George, into his broken magic hat of a condo in Hollywood. Everywhere in the place was dust, fading signed clippings, posters, the glory of his past. And everywhere were mirrors—and that made everything so much better.

She started to try and make a point to only look at him in reflection. And herself. That was her in the mirror, winking back at her. And that was the him everyone else saw, George Z. Tassell, a gorgeous, famous man, a magician, *hers.*

(Yes, he is yours. Yes. Your rat-headed man. And what are you?)

And then:

That Day.

A day after the night when he came home smelling of someone else, the scent of a honey-flower perfume and sex on him. And they drank cheap wine that night and she pretended she knew nothing of the someone-else smell, nothing of the Rat-Head, and nothing absolutely nothing of the voice in her mind.

And she drank and drank and he drank and drank and then they both slept and slept some more. The next day, That Day, it was hot. Flies were thick on the screen door. That Day they drank more cheap wine for breakfast ('hair of the dog') and walked around naked, flopped together, and walked around naked some more. How was it true, but they were happy—Yes? Yes? Happy? In the reflection, there he was, a truly handsome, beautiful man. And yet, staring at him directly, all she could see was that head–

She threw a dirty glass at that head. Yes.

George ducked, the mirror behind him shattered. And in her broken reflection she saw what she'd become.

He didn't ask why she had thrown it. He was so shocked he could not even find that question. And she hypnotized him immediately with her magic words: *I want you inside me.* When he came inside her, she—winding herself around him—she said it again and again and again. And then he slept in her arms, and she looked down at his sleeping face. Yes. She would take that inside her, too.

He had the head of a rat, but she had the mind of a snake.

She dislocated her jaw and took his Rat-Head into her mouth.

And then she slowly swallowed him

whole.

THE CAUSE

Part 1: Dead Love and Dirty Cash

I was looking to get a word from my kid, instead I got news there'd be no more words. He had been unceremoniously popped and what of it?

What was I gonna do about it?

His name was Theo P. The kids in the neighborhood called him "The Fish," but I insisted on calling him by his given name. He was one of my better and long-trained squeals in the Fairfax district, but still only fourteen years old. Train a kid for years to survive it all and then he gets popped in some random raid. It happens, and more and more in this day and age. Old house on the hill folks live what seems like forever while the God-Knock street kids regularly take the dirt dive for a look sideways at the wrong Syg-man in uniform.

Sure, it happens, but it hurt more than I was used to.

There was nothing to do about it because I was nothing but a shadow in this world anyhow. Nothing to do but buy a bottle and start on it as I took the scenic route back to the office, feeling damn sorry about everything this crummy world had given and taken.

Theo P. was a kid who cracked wise. He appreciated my style the way only a kid can—by imitating it and then going for it harder. He wore a suit *and* a fedora. He studied the phrases and would teach them to me, come up with new words and new slang. He was the one who started calling himself and his types 'squeals.' He had a memory for everything—facts, figures, dates, visuals—and he could sing or speak out what he'd figured out so you wished you could remember things, too.

I found him when he was seven, barely up to my waist in height. He was trying to hustle me into some cubes of Slack. When I wasn't interested in that, he wanted to get me down for some hot synthetics and prosthetics. He was funny about it. He told me he didn't know the last time I looked in the mirror, but I could use a better nose and maybe a good night's sleep. I told him he could use a better job, and he said, didn't he know it.

I bought him lunch and started training him. He ribbed me a lot about the way I dressed, the way I talked, and the way I paid in cash. But even as he was ribbing me I could see he was a bit in awe of it. It gave him an idea of something else he could be.

The kid was whip-smart, and he liked history: Civil War battles, Protestant Revolution, French Revolution. He particularly loved the tales of workers from the Industrial Revolution, especially the Luddites. He called me "Ludd," which I knew coming from him was a real compliment.

"Ludd" was how they all got to know me in the Fairfax district, thanks to Theo P. I was pretty sure he was gonna get radicalized when he hit his later teens, met the right God-Knock, and he'd start trying to destroy the machines. Dying for a cause and being remembered. That was written all over him. But he died just because, just because he happened to be walking when some sprays of bullets went flying. That was beyond tragedy. That was the sort of thing that let you know that nothing mattered anyhow, anyway.

When I made it back to the office, she was waiting for me.

I was pretty much as she had left me two decades before, weepy-eyed and stinking of Jack.

She wasn't the type to keep it to herself.

"Well, I guess there's comfort that some things don't change," she said.

"Don't fix what ain't broke," I said, thinking she was commenting on the suit, the tie, a bottle in a paper bag and an old school smoke, straight outta last century and what of it? I've made a point of blank refusal of this hyper-drive into hyper-space hyperbolic brave new world, and it's kept me cool when everything else on the planet's overheating, so I took it as a compliment.

But truth was, I didn't match her to her face or that cut to her voice. She wasn't anybody I thought I'd met before. That's how different she was. Then again, when I woke up some mornings, that's the way I felt about this whole goddamned city.

So I took a long look at her, then a swig from my bottle in the brown paper and licked my lips a little and then grimaced at the picture she presented.

A pretty woman is a complex system of problems. Because a pretty woman only has as much power as she has pretty—and that's like oil and water and kind hearts—a dwindling resource. She was a sunset. Everything was lighting up the most beautiful it would ever be again before it faded. You knew it wouldn't last much longer. Look while you could.

So I looked.

And she liked the way I looked at her because she started to glow with it.

"Hank, it's me," she said. "Danika." And her hand touched mine.

And it came back like a fever.

I remember touching her skin, her arms, her face. Her thighs wrapped around me. A look in her gray eyes, pupils large and rolling, her mouth an open O, her hair red and falling over both of our faces like a curtain.

I remember her saying, "I need you," "Don't leave me," and "Help." I remember punching someone, blood on my knuckles from his nose, my hand hurting.

I remember falling in love and then I remember her saying goodbye. It couldn't have been more than a month we were together. Maybe two.

I remember the cascade of her voice and how I loved it when she told me stories. What stories? What did she tell me?

I remember...

But maybe I don't.

Where are those drives? Where are those files? It was before everything was in the clouds on the drives in the sky, before everything rained down on us all in a storm. Before everyone let the machines beneath their skin, everyone but the God-Knocks, the Anarchists and me. Before, when we all knew, whether we believed it or not, that we were going to die.

And we still could remember on our own.

I am still trying to remember on my own. It makes me an anomaly to try. It also makes me a fool to try because I drink too much.

Her perfume was different now but beneath it was her same smell. That smell was bringing me to where we were when she left. Yes. Drunk and teary.

She was leaving.

"Why?" I had asked.

She hadn't had an answer.

And here we were again, only this time I wasn't crying over her. I put a hand to my temple. "So," I finally mustered, "what brought you here?"

"I need your help," she said.

"Ah, I seem to recall that getting you help got me into some trouble before."

She told me how different she is now, of course, can't I

see it? She smiled. "We create our lives, Hank."

Ah. Then I knew. She'd become one of *them*:

"Singularity Knowledge—unity in higher thought and immortality."

The Sygs. Our new enlightened ruling class. With their prosthetics and their Tatts and their insufferable positive-speak.

She told me how amazing her life was now, with this newfound power. How she did all this, attracting it with her powerful mind and the force of Singularity Knowledge in practice. Her husband was 95 years old but still very healthy with all his synthetics and prosthetics and probably could screw her harder than he could when he was 35.

She has manifested the life she wanted, she said.

But I knew she just married it. And then when her legally bound John moves

along to the great drive in the sky she will get to keep what she never earned, just like it's been happening for eons. Same story, she'd just updated it with the new religion, and the irony was with his new implants she might move along before him. What a joke. I thought maybe I'd make that joke. But I didn't because there was something about seeing those creases in her eyes that got me kind of liquid in the chest.

When I first knew Danika she was practically a kid, calling herself 'Dandy' and she stripped in bars for cash, back when people still used it. People would put their dirty paper in her underwear and that's how she got paid. Demeaning times for women and for everyone, so we were all glad to salute the Syg Flag and say thank you for all the awareness training that makes the elite fit to rule and saps like me drooling infants that need everything monitored, measured and analyzed. But don't mistake me as bitter. I wasn't then.

I didn't have the Tatt but it wasn't because of religious differences like the backwoodsy God-Knocks. I'd just learned to be suspicious. And in my line of work, it helped to not be so... visible. I guess I was old-fashioned. You'd be surprised at how effective a detective that made me in this day and age.

Which I guess is why Dandy—excuse me, she'd been Danika for over a decade now—was asking me for help.

"What do you want?" I asked her. I tried to growl, but it came out like a whimper.

She wanted me to find the killer of her lover, Lancaster J. He'd gotten a shaft of metal through the chest while sleeping in his bed. They'd had a date planned for a day later and when he hadn't shown she'd gone to his place and found him like that. She'd called in the cops who'd scuttled the place back and forth, she'd called media who squawked some real colorful stories, but it was all just noise. No one knew who stuck him, so whoever did it either had no Tatt or knew how to keep their fingers clean.

She was tired of waiting and tired of getting theories on her feed that went nowhere. She wanted answers. Who would do such a thing to a musician, an artist, already almost immortal for his beauty and his brilliance? She was still so in love with this dead man I almost wished I could kill him again.

She put down three hyper-drives on my desk.

Based on the rock she had on her hand, my first suspect was her husband, but she brushed that away. They had an arrangement, she said, and had for years. He wasn't the jealous type. He was the one who suggested she find me; he was the one who would be paying my bill. Her husband suggested me because I got a reputation with all the old codgers whose parents were alive when black and white movies were the norm. They appreciated the anomaly of a work-for-hire who brought my level of nostalgia to the table. I shrugged. Maybe I wasn't even who I thought I was, just some marketing scheme I'd dreamed up and was living out.

It was possible. That I was living it out so well I'd forgotten I'd ever even dreamt it up in the first place. That was damn near too likely.

"When he recommended my services, did he know about us?" I asked.

She seemed confused so I clarified our carnal history for her recollection.

She brushed a wisp of hair from her face. It was not red anymore; it was not a curtain. It was now blonde and piled on the top of her head like a crown. She used polite and affirming terms but assured me that our history was so inconsequential as to be nothing her husband cares to know about.

"But he cares to know about your lover and who stuck him?"

"Lancaster was important to everyone," she said, her eyes misting up. "He was going to be somebody and do something important."

"Sure he was," I said. "I'm sure he was gonna do something real swell."

She didn't like that.

"Let me tell you something," she says. "You think this performance of yours, this living like you're some detective out of the nineteen-hundred forties black and white movies makes you special?"

"Your husband seems to think so."

She ignored that and went straight to inspirational Syg-talk.

"Why make yourself a character in a world that's dead?" she asked. "Especially now, when we are so close to being able to live forever?"

"Oh, not everyone will get to live forever," I replied. "Just rich assholes."

"Rich assholes that pay your tab," she spit at me.

"So pay it," I said. "Or just *accept* your dead lover and get back to your holier than thou Syg-life."

She sighed then. Real pretty like, and sad. She nodded her head. "I'll pay it. You find who killed him, I'll pay the amount you want."

She held out her hand. On the back of it was a rose—one of the newest styles.

I shook my head. I swigged out of the bottle.

"I don't do the Tatt. Just cash."

"Cash? Are you kidding?"

"Nope. It's nothing but green."

She talked a bit about how that'd take time to get, and I told her it was her clock ticking, not mine. I just had this bottle to drink, is all. She asked me what I had against the Tatts—this amazing way of making commerce and memory flow seamlessly.

"Just old-fashioned enough to think getting branded and tagged makes you a target for slavery or extermination."

She laughed in a hard sort of way.

"Old-fashioned. That's a nice way of putting it."

"I got a million nice ways."

"Sure you do."

I got up close then, leaning in like I was ready to kiss her. "You remember some of them."

"I'm sure I don't," she said. "And you smell like a drunk beggar."

I'd been called worse. I kept close. I touched the rose with my fingertips.

"Not having it doesn't mean you're invisible, you know," she said. "It just means that you can have everything you own stolen."

I touched her Tatt to my lips. I said something about how I remembered how she used to be pretty fond of cash.

And then I made a joke that it was only fitting, considering her history, that she put that cash in my underwear.

She pulled her hand away from my lips and gave me a quick slap to the face.

She called me a drunk again and asked if I was taking the case or just going to continue to embarrass myself.

I said I'd do both.

She left then, leaving me the drives to see what I could see of her dead lover's mind.

Part 2: Memory and the Machine

I got the system to read the drives. No work for hire could live without 'em, and I figured I'd finish what was left in the bottle and then go cold turkey the next day. Tomorrow, right? That was always the best day to start. Right then, a little Jack would help me walk through another man's memories.

Lancaster J's thoughts came up on the walls in thumbnails I could touch and expand into three dimensions, and I was in a room of ghosts.

Thumbnails. You could leave them with fingerprints when you have the Tatt. Everything you'd see becoming something someone else can sift through, anyone with access could be inside your first person.

Being inside Lancaster J. was as good as any drug. If only I was actually him instead of me, I wouldn't have needed to finish the bottle of Jack.

Memory—this was our new contested ground. What we thought, what we remembered. How do you fight for what's in your own mind?

One of Theo P's best raps, and he could crack it sharp, was the story of the Luddites. I never remembered all the lines or the way he made it rhyme, but he had it down like a history lesson. He had the characters, the dates, the marches, the executions, the attention to sensory details and the rallying cause to give it an inspiring air. He told how the Luddites were heroes demanding living wages for skilled labor, warning against becoming mechanical in heart and mind, and he would end with a chorus of something like, *"Bring the hammer down, and if you have no hammer, throw your body on the machine!"*

The God-Knocks in the neighborhood ate it up. Someone down there might still remember how it went.

And then as I was watching Lancaster J's memories, thinking of memory and the machine, suddenly I realized I've let one play for too long and she was there again, in the room with me. It wasn't really her, of course. It was his memory of her. Her eyes were more blue than gray. She was smiling in a way I'd never seen her smile. The way she looked at me made me feel like there was hope for me after all. That I was more than shark chum in the human highway rapidly moving toward both immortality and extinction. These were new visions, but really it was all just the same story that had always been told. Boy meets girl.

But of course, she wasn't looking at me. She was looking at him.

That's the thing about these memories. These first person camera eyes we have. Even knowing—knowing all along she's looking at him—I watch it and it feels like she's looking at me.

Me me me me me me me.

I turned it off and stared out my window, past drunk now.

No one was gonna bring in three hyper-drives of Theo P's loves, thoughts, snapshots his mind took. Theo P. was somebody important. He was going to do something important, more than this Syg gigolo, Lancaster J., whose head I was in. That no one would remember Theo P. was wrong in a way I had never felt anything was wrong before. I had to do him some homage. Something.

But I was stumbling, falling into a blackness. I'd succeeded then in blotting out my own mind. My last thought before it all faded to black:

"Tomorrow I am going to stop drinking."

I dreamt she came back in that sharp darkness. She made slow love to me again, both as Dandy and Danika, telling me the new technology writes everything inside the skin so it's invisible. She did it while I was sleeping so I couldn't refuse. "It will make it all so much easier, better," she said. Then she told me she took the liberty of having the Tatt made as her name and placed in the skin above my heart. Now all business will be so much more convenient.

I woke up from the dream with it still dark outside, mad because everything hurt and the dream was too on the nose to even be interesting. Was that dream mine? Hers? Lancaster's? It felt like my poor brain cranking itself, trying to ask my poor heart to feel again. The dream was a gift, though, because I realized I didn't have it anymore. That liquid in my heart was crusty and dry. I was alone, still drunk and Theo P. was still popped with not a person to say boo about it.

Then I had a real diamond of an idea. I knew what I'd do, and I knew how to fix it all. All it took was my losing a piece of conscience to gain some sense of righteousness. I could suddenly understand the appeal of all the Sygs, the God-Knocks, the whole history of anyone who'd ever had a religion they'd kill or die for.

I had a cause.

I knew what to do.

I'd plant a memory in Lancaster's hyper-drive. I knew an Anarchist hacker who could do anything in the hyper-world, who'd do it just to do it. But I'd give her some of the dirty green paper when I got it just to make it real sweet.

I'd plant a memory and frame an innocent kid. It would make everyone stand up and pay attention. Oh, it was going to be beautiful. What a story I could put together, a poor God-Knocking street kid, radicalized to murder.

I practiced announcing my findings a couple of times just because it felt so good to say it, like a lullaby to get myself back to sleep.

"Danika," I'd say, "I found your killer. His name is Theo Pescadora. They call him *The Fish*."

In the contested battle I'd have thrown Theo P's body on the machine.

He'd be remembered.

And to be remembered as a villain is as good as being remembered as a hero.

Maybe better.

Part 3: Tomorrow

I woke up later that day, remembering my plan but my eyes were seeing nothing but white, and it felt like a hammer was inside the machine of my head pounding out, threatening to, at last, bust it wide open.

I remembered also that Today was Tomorrow, the day I would stop drinking.

I braved daylight. I went back to the Fairfax district. I was like a Robespierre there in my suit and pasty skin, accepted like a moving historic landmark. Everything was too bright, too loud, too tight. When was night going to fall? This day had already been too damn long and maybe it was time I gave up on it. When was that sun going to set?

Kid C.—only twelve and already with the bug eyes of someone who smoked the Slack that was all the rage—was standing looking up at the traffic going back and forth in the sky.

"Hey Ludd," he called, too loud. "You looking for a new squeal?"

I tried for it. "Do you know who popped Theo P.?" I asked.

"Nope," he says. "Nobody knows nothing. You know how it is."

Then I noticed on the back of Kid C's hand, as bright and shiny as a new sore, a big rose tattoo.

"When'd you get that?" I asked.

He was proud. "Just got it!"

Tatts are rare in the Fairfax district. It's crawling with God-Knocks, and they refuse it with old-school religious conviction as the sign of the Beast from the Good Book.

"Why'd you go and do a thing like that?" I asked.

He gave me a real 'smile for the camera' type grin. Then he looked back up into the sky at the traffic. "Ludd, man. You old."

We just stood there a while, me staring at this kid, him staring at the sky, me thinking about Lancaster J., Dandy, Theo P., but most of all, how I need a drink, I need a drink, dear God, I need a drink.

Tomorrow I'd go talk to my Anarchist friend.

Tomorrow I'd call Dandy back and start putting out the breadcrumbs to lead us to a murderer, a memorial I'd make to the kid, Theo P., a martyr to the cause.

To the cause.

What was the cause again?

God, my head hurt. Every thought. Hurt.

Tomorrow. Today I was going to finish the bender I started the day before. Today I was going to get so drunk I forgot who I was or why.

I turned around and walked away.

Kid C. called after me, "Wait, Ludd! I can help! I can figure it out! Just give me a mystery!"

I stopped. I felt something in my heart pushing against my chest, some dam behind my eyes threatening to burst. I walked back to the kid.

"Help me with this mystery," I said to him, my voice soft and shaking. "What are people *for*? Tell me that, kid…what *are* we?"

The kid looked at me straight a moment.

"Oh, that's easy," the kid said. And then he started laughing.

I waited for him to say more, but he was so high he just laughed and kept laughing.

I walked away and something broke in me for good as I got it.

No mystery. Just a big joke.

HAPPY HOUR

It was south of 6 p.m. at the Lamplite Inn. The working stiffs were loosening their ties and lips as they made the most of the last of happy hour.

He was one of those stiffs who very much wanted to forget that he'd spent his day doing "data compilation" and resenting his superiors. He snubbed their expensive watering hole with atmosphere for the Lamplite—a no frills place to get sloshed on the cheap. You got darts, a crappy old jukebox and ugly bartenders. Cash only. Stiff drinks.

He was into his second drink when she walked in, a pretty wisp of a thing with straight brown hair, a gray sweater and a knee length skirt that showed just how perfectly put together she was. He might have whistled a little under his breath and watched her, the way the rest of the ruffians and stiffs watched her, as she took a seat near the end of the bar with empty stools all around. They were all sure to swarm suddenly, so he thought he better pre-empt them. He'd never been afraid to have a pretty lady insult him, so what the hell.

"Can I buy you a drink?" he asked.

Her fingers had been playing with a clasp on a small handbag, but they stopped. "That would be lovely," she said, her voice as light and sweet as a buttermint.

He flagged the bartender, who had a well lived-in face, and deeply exposed leathery cleavage.

"What'll it be?" the bartender asked, in a tone like a threat.

"Whiskey, rocks," the young lady said.

"The well, okay?"

"The well is fine," the girl said.

He interrupted—knowing the well was certainly not fine—and ordered a proper label drink for her. The girl politely accepted the upgrade.

"My name is William," he said.

"Lily," she said, extending a small, white hand to him. He took it and shook it. His heart flopped over like a dog begging for a tummy rub.

The bartender brought her drink, and Lily sipped it while he tried to think of what to say. It left his mouth before he could swallow his tongue to stop it:

"What's a nice girl like you doing in a place like this?"

She didn't answer. He knew he had blown it. Sport a dumb line like that once and that's all you get. She was already looking around as if searching for another place to sit. She took a large gulp of her drink and then looked him in the eyes. Hers were deep, deep brown, reminding him of those belonging to a movie star whose name he would never remember.

"That's a bit of an existential question, don't you think?" she answered. Pretty *and* educated. Uh-oh.

He shrugged. He'd never been smart, and wouldn't even dare to pretend to be. "You just seem nice, is all," he said. He knew he should just walk away now with his tail between his legs.

"I used to be," she said. "I worked very hard to be a very good, moral person, to be a good example to my younger siblings. I am the oldest of six, so I wanted to make sure I only made decisions I would be comfortable with them emulating."

Big family. That meant Catholic or Mormon. She was in a bar, so that should eliminate Mormon.

"Catholic?" he asked.

"Yes."

"Still?"

"Oh, yes. Nothing like being exorcised to really solidify one's Catholic faith."

"Huh?" He hadn't heard her right, obviously.

"Are you trying to pick me up?" she asked, straight up.

He could only respond with the truth. "Well, yeah."

"Well, then you should know before you proceed trying to pick me up what it is that you're trying to lift."

"Ohhhkay," he stammered. She talked straight but he could still barely follow.

She was beautiful, she drank whiskey and he was pretty sure he was head over heels in love already.

"I used to be a 'nice girl.' Then I got raped by a demon."

He wasn't certain where the lower half of his jaw was but he felt a definite breeze drying the inside of his mouth. He couldn't properly clear his throat, nor look away. It was a long moment, but it was definitely his turn to say something.

"Whoa," he said. "Bummer."

She shrugged her narrow shoulders and stared off ahead of her. Her voice was sweet and soft. "Yes."

"Uh, well…huh. Are you okay? Now?"

She gave him half a smile that was so much like the first touch of sunlight after a season of storms that he had to watch it and see if it would warm the sky. "I am okay. Thank you."

His mouth found its bottom half and his teeth clanked together. He knew he should move away now, run away, even.

But she was so pretty. And her drink was empty.

He ordered her another one.

They made small talk. She grew up in a rural town in the middle of the country. She came to this city to work because she had wanted a fresh start, and she liked the skyline. He told her he lived a few blocks over, and she relayed that she was working as a receptionist two streets south. He couldn't help thinking that it only made sense for it to be *his* place if he got as far as a "my place or yours" toss-up. But of course, a girl this assorted box of nuts—he couldn't afford the kind of dental work cracking that would cost.

But he was tempted to try. This beautiful girl seemed to genuinely enjoy his company—something just short of a miracle these days. He'd been down on his luck with a barely serviceable job (but thankful for a job all the same) and what felt like few prospects. He was not a handsome man. He'd been called "ugly" within earshot enough to have few illusions about that. But he worked out, tried to eat right, and used quality personal grooming products. He'd never be a catch, but he was a decent guy. A guy other guys liked to have around and a guy girls liked to have as a friend.

He'd had girlfriends, one he even thought might lead to marriage. But that had just ended recently and nastily. And this girl, Lily, was the prettiest girl who had ever given him this much of her time. And even if she had just told him something crazy, she didn't *seem* crazy, not at all. In fact, she seemed so down-to-earth that he found himself wondering if he hadn't just imagined her reply to his pick-up line. But then again, he never had much of an imagination.

"Do you have a boyfriend?" he asked.

She shook her head.

"Pretty girl like you without a boyfriend?"

She laughed. "Yeah. Go figure, but the whole being raped by a demon, possessed and exorcised seems to be a bit of a turn off."

He nodded his head. That made sense. What didn't make sense is that she

shared this story in the first place. "Why do you tell people?"

"Because if someone's worth my time, they're worth the truth. If someone wants to get involved with me, they should know what they're dealing with."

She had no malice in her eyes or half-smile on her lips, so it was obvious she wasn't trying to play some joke on him for some secret dare or her own amusement. It was clear to him that she believed what she said, even though it was hard to imagine anyone else would.

"Well, so, people believe you when you say all that… stuff…happened to you?"

"I wouldn't say that."

"But you still keep saying it."

"I've been through a lot, and I don't believe in lying about it or pretending it didn't happen just because other people don't believe it."

Damn. She knew how to make it seem like she was making sense. "So…you were possessed?"

She nodded. "Yes. For about a year and a half."

"And then, you got an exorcism?"

"Yes."

"And that worked?"

"Eventually."

"So, how long have you been…clean?"

"About two years."

"And you haven't had a boyfriend since then?"

She shook her head. "Still not back in the saddle, so to speak."

"But you're…cured, right? You're not going to get possessed again?" he asked, remembering that there was definitely more than one Exorcist movie.

"The Bible says something that scares me."

That the Bible said something that scared her, scared him. How religious was this girl? How totally bonkers? How was he still sitting there?

She had finished another drink.

She stared at her empty glass, but also seemed to be staring into space. This was it, his cue to excuse himself and run for the hills.

"So, how did it happen?" He had never been good at taking cues.

She turned her doll-like face to him, her eyes registering him as if just remembering he was there, but there was a gratitude in them as well, that he was there and had not disappeared. His heart flopped over again.

"I was at school. I got this amazing scholarship and I was sent on a full ride to this elite women's college. My mom didn't want me to go. She was worried that I would become a lesbian, or fall away from the faith, or fall in love with a Protestant, or any number of things that seemed terrible to her at the time. So, she worried a lot, but she certainly didn't worry about what actually happened. That's a funny thing about worry, you know? She was worried about the big, wide liberal elite, when what she should have been worried about was the unleashed powers of hell. You'd think as a devout Catholic she would have thought of it more literally.

"Anyway, there I am, a freshman on a full ride scholarship at a private school, feeling on top of the world. My brain is taking in all these amazing classes and lectures and all the people seem so cool and interesting and I am excelling at everything. Thriving. I got straight A's my first semester. I was involved in clubs and nonprofit work. My professors liked me, my classmates liked me, everything seemed in bloom. I had never been more happy.

"So, second semester, a couple of weeks before midterms, my roommate is staying over at her boyfriend's school, which happened fairly often. Suddenly, at exactly 3am, my eyes suddenly just open. There is a feeling of electricity running through my body. I don't know what's up…why I'm suddenly awake. But I hear something outside my room, in the dorm hall. A sound which I can only describe as coming from an animal being skinned alive. It was a terrible sound.

No one else on the hall seemed to notice, at least, no one was stirring. I got up and went to the door. There was nothing that I could see. Our dorm halls were lit, even at night, and it was totally empty.

"But then the light at the end of the hall started to flicker. The lights were those industrial kinds they have everywhere—the um, what are they called—?"

"Florescent lights?" he said.

"Yeah. Fluorescents, but there's another word. I can't remember now. It's not important. You know what kind of lights I mean—those long rectangular ones? Anyway, it starts flickering there at the end of the hall. I start walking toward it. I realize now, that was my mistake. It was calling me with that flickering, but I didn't know. I just started walking toward that flickering light, not really thinking, just moving.

"And I walk to the end of the hall, and the light flickering goes out. So now that end of the hallway, it's dark. And it's not even a second. Not even a full second that I feel this thing—I feel this chill—like—there's no way to describe it. It's not even like cold. More like shivers up and down your spine, but it's everywhere, all over, it's paralyzing, maybe it's fear itself, I don't know, but I couldn't move. I was frozen in place, and I was just staring at…

"At nothing. There was nothing there…just this terrible feeling and this light that just went out and that's it. And I am telling myself—because I think of myself as an intelligent person who is not at all superstitious, you know—that I just had a nightmare, and I am standing here in the hallway getting spooked by a light going out and the sound. Must have been, well, maybe I had a nightmare I couldn't remember. Who knows? But I am telling myself to move now, and my body listens and I start moving. Walking, now, back to my room. And I shut the door and I lock it and I think. Okay. I am okay. And I get back in bed.

"And then I see it. It is there, waiting for me in the darkness. This thing beyond description. This thing so hideously ugly you can't even imagine it. It's a huge upright goat-like thing covered with hair and what looks like scabs and sores. And it's got this huge, bifurcated penis that is erect.

"I scream as it leaps on me and pins me down with its hooves, which are pressing into my joints and bones, and I feel like they are breaking beneath its weight. Its yellow eyes are glowing and rolling back in its head as it tears apart my nightgown and claws down my heart, tearing into my breasts and belly. And then its two-headed cock-thing just pounds into me like two saws attached to a jack-hammer.

"And as much as I thrash or move or scream or struggle, the more it seems to enter me, to impale me, to gouge deeper and deeper into me and then just let loose this burning deluge of acid inside me.

"And I am screaming and screaming as this thing brutalizes my body, rapes me, twenty minutes, thirty minutes, an hour, it seems like four days and then finally, finally the door busts open and campus security is there. But I don't feel relief. After all this, I am sure that I am going to die and this thing will kill them, too. But then, just as I've accepted my impending death, this thing just…vanishes with the shadows as the lights come on."

William could hear the sound on the jukebox. It was Neil Diamond singing "Sweet Caroline." He had forgotten where they were.

He had forgotten to doubt. He suddenly remembered. "What did the security do?"

She shrugged, then started chewing on her lower lip. He felt that everything she said before, she said matter-of-fact, like she had said it so many times it had lost all meaning for her. But whatever happened to her next was somehow *worse* than that.

"Well, they see me," she continued. "They know *something* happened to me. I mean, my clothes are all tore up and ditto the bed, but they saw nothing of this thing. And that's the way it all gets looked at and reported—that they didn't see my perpetrator—and the more I tell them what this thing was, the more they start looking at me like I'm crazy. Well, I tell them the truth, I tell them everything. I tell the doctor the truth when he examines me. And the doctor—well, I should say doctors, there were many of them—they find, of course, that while they find I've been beaten up, what they don't find is human semen or human hairs or human anything. Neglecting the fact that the demon was clearly not human, so of course they wouldn't find anything human staining me, they decide if it isn't human, then it's nothing. So instead of believing me, they believe what they can, which is that I have had a psychotic breakdown.

"So, now, the word about campus is that I made this whole thing up. That I imagined this whole thing—that I tore up my own bed, clawed and brutalized myself. That I am sticking to this story of being raped by a demon to get attention, or because I'm losing my mind or because I was raised in a religious household in a world too enlightened for a bogey man, and that cognitive dissonance—there's a college word from my first semester—the *cognitive dissonance* from the way I was raised with the current academic philosophy of my environment helped exacerbate this mental breakdown. Such *bullshit.*" She put her face in her hands and started sobbing softly.

The bartender noticed that the intense conversation had turned into the lady crying. She looked at William with a "should I do something?" shrug. William quickly held up two fingers for two more drinks. He was way too sober.

The bartender put them down in front of them, prompting Lily to look up.

"Thank you," she said to the bartender, wiping her eyes and nose with the back of her gray sweater. And then to William, "Thank you. You are very kind. A real peach." She gave him a smile that turned him to liquid. "That's what they used to say in my grandma's time to say that you were really great. 'A real peach'."

William wasn't sure whether what was tugging at his heart was pity, compassion, or what. He wanted so badly to wrap himself around her small shoulders, he wanted to envelop her and tell her he'll protect her against the shadows.

"Did you leave school?"

"Sure did. I took the recommended leave of absence for medical and personal reasons. And I went home. And my family, they actually believed me. You can't imagine what a relief, what a wonderful, beautiful feeling it was to know the people I loved most in the world believed me."

He nodded. He wanted to believe her. He had never wanted to believe anything so much, fucked up as it is. But he didn't. He couldn't.

"And I was happy to be home," she continued. "But then…well, it started at night. I would wake up again and again at 3am, and I would feel it inside me, clawing at me, kicking at me, holding me down from the inside and ripping me up. The pain was unimaginable…terrible…I would faint from it. And I would start thrashing and screaming and going into fits. Then it started happening at any time, different times throughout the day. Everything starts to blend together, and I have a hard time remembering what happened when. I start forgetting what I'm doing. I would faint from the pain and black out and when I would come to, well, I would have done things. Terrible things."

"Like?"

"Well, I was apparently eating bugs, my own feces and urine. I sodomized myself with a votive candle and tried to do the same to my sister. One day, I came to and saw my mom's arm in a sling because I had thrown her across the room. I remembered nothing."

It's one thing to watch a movie with an actress spitting up green soup, and quite another to hear a girl you are hitting on tell you she ate her own shit. William wasn't sure what to do with the fantasy he had since they'd started talking of slowly kissing her with an open mouth. All of his desire, which had stayed just as hot even during her terrible story of the 'demon' forcing itself upon her, now distinctly chilled. He found himself looking elsewhere as she continued to speak.

"Of course, they called in Father Greenfield, our family priest. He's heard most every confession of mine and after hearing my mother's hushed 'there is something wrong with Lily, Father Greenfield,' he came over, expecting me to have a fever or something. Instead, I'm all eyes rolled back in my head, foaming at the mouth, thrashing against these belts my parents had used to tie me to the bed post to keep me from trying to kill myself or them.

"Now, they're already thinking exorcist, but they don't want to say that. They're still trying to keep the fact that their daughter was raped and is now possessed by a demon hush-hush because, obviously, in a small town that is not the sort of 'my daughter went off to college and guess what?' experience you want to relay. But Father Greenfield starts by going a completely different direction. He's a fairly scientific man for a Catholic priest, and figured there was a better explanation than that I had been raped and now possessed by a demon. So, he theorized that the goat-like thing was actually some sort of animal that had attacked me and that it, and now I, was suffering from rabies.

"Which is actually a really good theory. Leave it to the priest to come up with the most reasonable theory and the doctors the most damning one, huh?"

Of course! It made so much sense, William found himself wishing he'd thought of it. It made perfect sense. Of course that's what it was! He felt so relieved! Rabies. He'd never known anyone who'd had rabies before.

"So, where do I go but back to the doctor," she continued. "Anyway, doctors, doctors, specialists, doctors, and then more doctors. In the end, they don't find evidence of rabies."

"Really?" William asks, disappointed as hell. "They didn't? It totally sounds like rabies." It had to be rabies. Rabies is what allowed him to believe her, and of course, not believe her at the same time.

"The doctors still find nothing. And then more of them to still find more nothing. My parents raked up so many medical bills with this whole thing, they had to get a second and third mortgage on our home. Then the whole sub-prime thing made us lose our family homestead. And ironically, the exorcism that actually worked cost nothing…unless, I mean, you count a lifetime of being Catholic."

This girl is funny, William thought. She doesn't laugh or smile much, but she's got a real wit about her. He smiles at her, and she rewards him with a gentle look that says he's just given her a bouquet of flowers.

"So, I've been doing all the talking," she said. "I'm sorry for that. I certainly don't mean to dump this all on you. But you've said you were interested in me, and I am interested in you, too. So please, please, tell me more about yourself."

"Oh, I…no," he said, hoping she wasn't expecting him to talk about *his* life at this point. As frightening as her tale had been, his life, in comparison, he in comparison, seemed like reading the ingredients on a box of corn flakes.

"Do you have a girlfriend?" she asked.

"No. Nah. I mean, I did, but it's over now."

"What happened?"

"Oh, uh, well. She cheated on me with this guy and then

I was like, you know, really mad. But then I forgave her, and then we got back together, and then she dumped me and married somebody else. That was like a year ago…months ago. And I haven't been, you know, really *over* that. I mean I wasn't. I am now. I'm totally over it now."

"How did you get over it?"

"Oh, uh…just time I guess. And…I don't know… knowing there are other girls out there. I mean, the second you walked in here I kinda forgot she ever existed."

"You are so wonderfully kind, William. Really. I can't tell you how much I appreciate your sweet words."

"Ah, well. I mean it. I mean, you're something. *You're* the real peach, you know."

And then she blushed.

And he blushed, too.

"So," he said, trying to find words now to stop himself from jumping all over her with his tail wagging and drooling. "How did *you* get over it?"

He was immediately sorry that he brought it back up. He could tell that she was sorry, too.

"Well, I still wouldn't say I'm 'over' being raped. I don't think I'll ever be over that. I am certainly no longer possessed. But I didn't really get over that so much, either, as much as that thing got forcibly expelled from me."

He really didn't want to hear about it anymore. He really just wanted to get on with the flirting, and close this whole conversation and chalk up this chapter of her life to rabies. But he had brought it up again, he might as well let her finish it.

"You had an exorcism."

"Yes, but listen. I'm going to tell you this, and then, William, here's what I want you to do. When I'm done telling you, I want you to get up and walk away, no hard feelings—quite the opposite, I completely understand. Or, if after I have finished telling you, you still want to pick me up, I am ready to go wherever with you. I don't care if you believe the story or not, I just care that you know what I know, and that you are free to make a choice from there if you're interested. Okay?"

He nodded.

She took a deep breath, closed her eyes, and told the last part.

"Poor Father Greenfield. He wasn't at all equipped for this sort of thing, but he wanted to help me so badly. He wanted to save me. So he did all he could. Even if that meant learning the exorcism rites and bolstering his faith, getting sick, feeling like he himself was being haunted and hunted by whatever it was that had found me. But he fought, and it fought back. Months of this. Months and months.

"And I am out of my body, staring out that window, watching the grass grow in the spring and die in the fall, become covered in ice and then covered in snow. I can hear the sound beneath the grass of worms and maggots and ants. I can hear everything eating and being eaten. I see my body over in the corner of the room, belted down.

"And the last night, as Father Greenfield is chanting trying to expel the unclean spirit from me, the wolves that lived in the woods outside our house start to howl. I was always afraid of them growing up, but I wasn't afraid anymore. They were afraid of *me*, now. And the me that is by the window, staring out of it, loves these wolves now, loves them for their wild hungry selves, and I want to leave now and howl with them. They howl and howl and howl. They are calling me, too. I know my body is on the bed, screaming, but me—the me that is me—is staring out the window and I want to go so badly. And then the window shattered.

"Father Greenfield is shocked at the broken window, and I see him shudder with the icy wind that blows in. My body, on the bed, shudders from the cold. It is weak and can't last much longer. I could see all my bones. My skin was covered with scabs and sores. I was just this thing now, this object that had been filled with all the hate and ugly and bad things that could contain it and finally the container was too used and abused and spent. But that *thing* inside my body didn't want me to die, because then where would it go?

"Suddenly, I was hovering near the ceiling, like you would float in water, staring down at my body that was weighted in all this hate and evil. I felt so sorry for the poor thing. And for Father Greenfield, of course. He wasn't looking well. And I knew if I died it wouldn't be good for him. Not only because he would feel so badly about it, but because people would probably blame him. And maybe they'd be right. He wasn't helping my body get stronger with his exorcism ritual. He certainly wasn't helping that thing in me get healthy. He was killing it by killing me, though I don't know if he knew that. And I felt sorry for all his wasted efforts.

"The window had been broken open, and the light was starting to break and I knew that I could go now, through that window. And I knew that the thing would die inside me. But I just felt so sad. I didn't want to die. I didn't want that thing to win. I didn't want that priest to fail. And the thing was asleep now and so tired. And I wasn't tired at all. I wanted to howl.

"Father Greenfield was half-conscious, just reading passages from the Bible aloud, and he read this passage that I didn't even recognize: *'When the unclean spirit has gone out of a person, it wanders through waterless regions looking for a resting place, but not finding any.'*

"And I know—and I *know*—I can howl it out. I shove my spirit back in my body, and my spirit howls against it, pushing it, shoving it, forcing it out now. It's too tired to fight me. It will die with my body or go.

"So it goes. And I can feel the evil spirit leaving me, tired, to go look for a place to rest. And the light is breaking outside the broken window. I can see that light, and I know that I am free. And…I have been free since then."

At the Lamplite, the lights had dimmed, the drinks had returned to regular price, the working stiffs had morphed into the night crawlers.

The hour was getting late.

William had to decide, whether to ask her back to his place, or to thank her for her company and move on.

She knew he didn't believe her, but she didn't care. And he knew that some crazy-ass shit had gone down one way or another, but no, he didn't care. Hell yeah, he was still interested.

"So, do you want to go back to my place?" he asked, surprised that his voice is choked up, and there are tears in his eyes. This was maybe the strongest choice he has ever made in his life. He has made the decision, free and clear, to take a recovered-rabid, religious woman back to his cramped apartment and try and make love to her despite the terrifying visions she had placed in his head.

He was crying as he was deciding this, he thinks, because he just might love her, and she had given him that possibility by telling him all the worst things first.

But he didn't know that the worst was gathering like a storm in the night, and to be fair, for her it was only a small fear from the end of a Bible verse that now she'd just as soon forget.

"Yes, William. I want to go to your place. Yes, yes, yes."

He isn't handsome, but he's strong. He isn't smart, but he says what he thinks.

He is no match for the things that will wait crouching in the stillness of the dark for her, but he will see them. He will see them, he will fight, and he will lose.

But not tonight.

Tonight, they are happy.

Part Three:

heart

In the Desert

IN THE DESERT

"You Know It's Going to Be a Bad Day When:

#1—You wake up facedown on the pavement."

I am looking at the Mr. Maesta's menu, representing *"The Best Food in Holbrook."* The front features a list of ten bad day signifiers that I am finding very comforting, even though about half of the punch lines end with some riff on "Your wife." It's still early and it's already been a very bad day for me, one of the worst I can recall. But honestly, not anywhere as bad as any of these ten. I think that's the point. To let you know, as my dad says, that it could be worse.

When I awoke this morning at five, I was not facedown on the pavement. I was in the most comfortable bed in which I've ever slept, amid a world of gold pillows. I had the window open and I could smell pine and dew. I was in Flagstaff, Arizona at an Airbnb, which I had reserved as a leisurely halfway point on the 16-hour drive from Los Angeles to Ruidoso, New Mexico for my family reunion. That morning my host prepared a breakfast for me: homemade granola, berries, yogurt, coffee and a hard-boiled egg served on a pewter egg cup that held it like a trophy. I brought the egg on the road with me because I was so full, but I knew I would want it on the 8-hour drive ahead.

Two hours later, I ate that egg in my broken-down car, in my hour-long-wait for a tow truck. Then I drank as much water as my body could hold. I was in the middle of nowhere in the hot desert. I figured eating and drinking was the thing to do to stop panicking.

I sat in my car, trying to keep my head about me. I put the shiny, collapsible window shade up over the windshield to keep the sun from killing me. I kept eating. I ate the half-sandwich, the crumbs from yesterday's scone, the ghost-pepper potato chips, the pickle-flavored popcorn and a Clif Bar. When the woman from AAA called to ask if my tow truck had arrived yet, I said it hadn't but not to worry, I was "eating my feelings."

I needed to pee. I squatted by the side of the road, bare-assed on the overpass, but I crouched down too far and leaked on my pants. I should have been less concerned about privacy. There were no cars around for quite some time. I changed into a red cowgirl skirt I had in the trunk. And felt stupid.

This was no act of God. It was 100% my own damn fault I was stuck. It was so dumb that if I'd died I could be featured on those Darwin Awards. I had pulled over to get coffee at a "Genuine Indian Souvenirs" shop that boasted giant tee-pees and person-sized plastic dinosaurs. I even said to myself, "This is why it's great to travel alone. I can stop anywhere I want just because I want to!"

I pulled off the freeway and turned toward the "Genuine" shop. As I pulled into a parking spot, I slipped on my left shoe while applying the brake – I always drive barefoot on long drives. And in one of those thoughtless habitual moves, I slid into right shoe, taking my foot off the brake before I had come to a full stop. That's when I hit the curb, rode up on to it and "high-centered" my car (as my family would tell me, my bonehead move had a name). I apologized profusely to my car (I do things like that), but she looked okay when I got out, if maybe her bumper was a little dented. No sweat.

The place was deserted of people. Not in a weird ghost town sort of way—I'd seen plenty of those on the drive that morning, abandoned and graffitied souvenir stops littering the side of the lonesome highway like old desecrated bones. This one had several cars parked in front, but the main door was locked and the windows gated. Then I saw the big CLOSED sign. I walked around the building, and it looked like maybe there was a residence behind there? Maybe people lived there and hadn't opened for the day, it still being early? Or maybe it wasn't open on Sunday? I walked around a bit, unable to get a grip on the character of this place and figure out why it was closed but still had all these cars parked in front, and I bet I could write a good horror story starting with this scenario. I returned to my car and started to drive.

At that moment, I hadn't realized how badly I had screwed Ms. Thang, my good-as-gold, work horse of a little car, my token of being a real self-sufficient adult—I had made every payment even when I was out of work, I had paid her off and she was mine now, I took good care of her. And then this. Five miles after resuming my journey on the freeway—passing a fast truck and singing really loudly—I noticed she was making a God-awful sound as I pushed the gas. And that she was slowing down despite my pressing the accelerator. I thankfully made it on to the exit ramp, where my car gave out altogether. So I was standing in the middle of the exit lane with the door open and my foot on the brake to keep her from rolling back and trying to figure out how I could push and steer at the same time.

An SUV filled with young men pulled up behind me and helped me push her to the side. They offered taking me with them a mile to the Petrified Forest where I could call for help. I instantly had in my mind a clear image of how I'd said I would write a scary story on this trip, and these events could make a solid first few story beats leading to the terror I'd had in mind. It freaked me out. In fact, I decided I would avoid thinking about any possible horror story until I was absolutely safe and secure. And even if these young men had just saved me from being stuck in the middle of an exit overpass, I sure as shit was not about to get into an SUV with a bunch of strangers.

I told myself to keep my head screwed on straight. I made the call to AAA. The nearest town was Holbrook, Arizona, about an hour away, and they were sending a truck to tow me there. I called my sweetheart (who had said as I planned this trip, "I don't like the idea of you driving alone in the desert," to which I replied for the first and last time in my life, "tough titty"). I just needed to stay calm and figure this out and not descend into self-loathing quite yet. I had much left to do and needed all my wits. I called my brother S., who I knew was eight hours behind me on the same course to our family reunion.

But I couldn't stop crying anyway and praying for Ms. Thang in the hour I waited for the tow-truck. I kept caressing her dashboard and saying a mantra of apologies. I still couldn't believe that I'd done this, and I would say so out loud so she could hear me, that I couldn't, I just couldn't, leave her here, dead in the middle of nowhere, in the desert. The worst part was the feeling that I couldn't trust myself. That somewhere there was something sinister within me, trying to teach me a lesson.

The Creature is... Me

My brother S. had asked me initially to ride with him and his kids to our family reunion. They live in Southern California and could easily scoop me up so it made sense. But I hadn't wanted to do that.

I'd been saying for the past year that I needed to go on a Vision Quest or something. A hunger, a boredom, an ache ate away inside of me for the past year or two—pulling on me and making me feel like I'd *come a long way, baby*, sure, but which way was that? And was this really the direction I had meant to go? And was this *it*? Was this, really, my life? I'd wanted so much more, didn't I? But I was different then. And to be honest, I wasn't up for a real Vision Quest, anyway. A sweat lodge, I would do that at some point soon, for sure—just like the other thousand things on my list I would definitely do at some point (things like…fix my typewriters, learn to tango, ride horses).

Our family reunion, which happens every few years in a different location, was looking like my only chance for a real vacation this year. I would settle for a road trip, self-actualization while driving solo, pondering my life as Ms. Thang and I made our way across the plains of the Great American Southwest. It would be my own sort of Vision Quest. No drugs. No spirit guides. Just me and my car.

Thus, I declined my brother's request and reserved a beautiful Airbnb in Flagstaff as my midway point.

Plus, I had one more short story I needed to write to finish my collection. I already knew the story would be called "In the Desert" after one of my favorite poems, and I already knew it had to be the heart of the collection. But I needed time with it, as I only had the naked bones. I knew there would be something fantastical and horrible that happens where the narrator's car breaks down in the middle of the desert. She makes the dumb decision to leave her car and walk toward a ghost town. It shimmers, like a mirage, in the sweltering heat, but eventually she makes it. It is empty during the day, but at night it comes alive with all these ghosts. She falls in love with the ghosts, and the place, but she knows she has to get out. Then at the end, as she tries to escape, she sees a grotesque, naked creature eating her own heart out. Then the twist: Surprise! The creature is actually just a reflection of herself—in a mirror.

A 16-hour car trip would be a good way to get some

thinking done on the flesh of the story, not to mention the week I would have at the family reunion, with a private room, where I could get down to business writing this thing. Sure, I'd have to beg off some festivities, but might it not be good to have an excuse like that? Might it make me seem more like a real and serious writer to my family members? They don't really know much about what I write, but they understand deadlines. ("Oh, she can't join us in the game of pinochle because she has to finish a story to get to her publisher.") All of my family members are supportive of me as a writer, but most of them haven't read much of my stuff because of all the motherfucking profanity I use. My mother is the only one who reads it all and even professes to like it.

For someone whom they all consider to be a 'free spirit,' I am more beholden to what they think of me than they'd imagine. They are all fun, brilliant people who are wonderful parents and have wonderful families and are real contributing-to-society adults. Me...well...I have a couple of cats. And I'm still living the dream, I suppose. I've come a long way. Used to be, I was a real mess.

The last time I had driven myself to New Mexico had been more than a decade ago. I had taken that trip to think about my disintegrating marriage while escaping L.A. for a while. My heart was broken, a sharp-edged, raw exposed thing, pumping only enough to get me to a place where I could think clearly. I quit my job, left my apartment and my cats with my soon-to-be-ex, and took off.

I knew there was a chance that I might not come back.

I had driven my same little car, and she had been so reliable and strong. She'd been shiny new back then.

On that trip, I would also write the draft of what would become my first novel.

Two months with my mom in New Mexico, writing a story about ghosts and love, reading new age self-help books and making my own holy water, doing blessings, and trying to change my way of thinking and hanging out with one of my high school friends who was still stuck there. That's how I found the bare bones of self. That time in the desert had healed me and I returned to L.A. and started creating a different life for myself. But I'd been lucky.

There are more ways to die than live in the desert.

What Would Stephen King Write?

So, it's hour two in Holbrook, Arizona where I am waiting for my brother to arrive like the Cavalry. I am holding an ugly floral umbrella because the sun is merciless, a jug of water that I'm downing like...water, and my backpack. It is Sunday in this small town and most everything, including the repair shop where my car is awaiting diagnosis, is closed. Nothing to do but see what this place has to offer.

As I walk in the baking heat, there is that terrible sweet smell of something dead and rotting. It is coming from an alley. I look to locate the source and find it. It is a dead white cat, and it is bloated with maggots. I avert my gaze, not wanting to remember my beloved childhood pet, a white cat with one totally green eye while the other was split across the middle with green on one side and blue on the other. My eldest sister, B., named her "Demi," referencing the half-colored eye. I was in love with that cat. She was *my* cat back in the Utah home, the home I shared with all seven of my siblings and my still-married parents, the home I still dream about regularly. I used to try to stop dreaming about being back in that house, floating in and out of rooms like a ghost, because it didn't feel psychologically healthy. I tried to start dreaming of burning it down, but that didn't work.

After my parents got divorced, Demi and I and my mom and the younger half of my siblings moved to New Mexico.

Within the first month, Demi ran away and I never saw her again. I always assumed she was trying to find her way back to the Utah home. I know this dead cat cannot be Demi, but I can't help but imagine this must be how she ended up somewhere, somehow, a victim of the desert while searching for her home.

I walk across the road to the other side of the street.

Some places look open over there, which I've learned can only be confirmed by testing the front doors.

The Holbrook Tourism Center and Museum is a huge brick building, bold and refined, as out of place in this town as a white wedding dress at a rodeo. It bears the only greenery in town, a lush lawn with some large trees providing the only shade for miles. I approach the front doors, expecting it to be closed, and lo and behold it is open. Inside it is cool, not air-conditioned but a relief of moderate temperature, and the whirr of fans sound like wings.

The Tourism Center and Museum used to be the area's only courthouse, and it has a small jail attached. They haven't altered the place much, except to create exhibits with artifacts and pictures on the wall. My eyes are first caught by huge chunks of petrified wood and fossils collected from the area. Weird salamander type mud-casts of creatures that were common when this area was under water during the time of the dinosaurs. I see old court documents, newspaper articles, Pony Express leather satchels. There are collections of personal items including 100-year-old dresses, photos and sundry kitchen supplies that belonged to descendants of the town's settlers who have donated them. There are typewritten descriptions of what time used to be like here. I feel like time hasn't changed much at all.

As I enter the old jail, I imagine what it must be like to be really trapped here, to be in a cell surrounded by bars and a dirt floor beneath your feet. Strange that there is detailed graffiti on the walls. One exceptional piece portrays the Virgin de Guadalupe with a face like a real person, against the background of a hemp leaf. There are elaborate nametags, poetry done in calligraphy. I don't tag the wall, but I do make sure I sign into the guest book.

I have this nagging voice that tells me to leave a trail.

But walking through the museum feels comforting, all the same. People made lives here in this desert, and have left and preserved all these pretty scraps behind glass cases. I walk slowly, slowly. I look at things twice. I talk to the woman behind the desk and ask questions about the fossils. I don't really want to leave because I feel safe here.

"Mr. Maesta's, The Best Food in Holbrook." I end up here with another four hours to kill. Being the only eatery open on Sunday it is really crowded, but I insist they have no need to serve me quickly as I will be there for a while. I eat fry bread, a Navajo taco (like a tostado except with more chili and pinto beans), and I drink six diet cokes. The place is filled with souvenirs and trinkets and weird cutouts of the Beatles, historic lunch pails, pictures of JFK. Random stuff that makes me at home.

I make an odd request of the waitress for some paper, and she brings me a sheet of the lined sort from her son who is doing his math homework in the back. I fill up the first page quickly and beg for more and her son delivers it himself with a shy, serious sort of gaze.

"I'm a writer stuck here without paper," I explain to him. "You're really helping a story out."

I write page after page. I write about the first day of my journey, my sojourn in Flagstaff, and how good it had felt then to be me. How I could watch words float across my mind like clouds. How the words in my head created this other self that I could dialogue with. How I could make myself laugh. But then I write this:

"Maybe this story is writing me."

I have to stop. I put down the pen.

I stop myself from thinking about all the ways I already could be dead.

I stop myself from thinking about all the ways I said to myself before this trip that it was *okay* if I died. I don't know why I do that. But I do. I tell myself what a good life I've had so far and that *it's okay, really*, if I die. Maybe better, even, because then I won't have to keep doing so much. I won't have to keep feeling terrible about being part of this whole human thing. I'll stop feeling like there is all this shit I still have to do that I haven't even touched yet. Like the dream I had last night where I was in the Utah home, and I realized that there were a bunch of rooms I had to clean and I'd only just started on my room. I guess I receive some sort of comfort thinking *it's okay if I die*. Like it will be a relief. Or maybe it is just my trying to pretend I'm okay with the inevitable.

But being here in the desert, I don't think it's okay at all. Not only do I want to live, I want to live *my* life, my life the way I have been living it. My life that feels uniquely and perfectly mine. Not by accident, by intense effort.

In my abandoned car, in her trunk, there is my yoga mat, there is a box filled with copies of my latest novel. My car, my yoga mat, my books. All intensely MINE.

In the glove compartment there lies all the necessary paper work, but also pictures of me and my friend on a trip, a toothbrush, tampons, random papers with story ideas and little rocks I collect. I leave my words everywhere like droppings. I leave a trail.

On post-it notes, on scraps of paper.

Mine, this moment. I am here, now. Me. Telling my story. Telling the lady at the historical museum, the tow truck driver, the lined pages of some child's homework that

I fill out at Mr. Maesta's. Because I am *here* and if so, then I want every *here* to be some sort of home.

But no.

No, I don't want Holbrook to be home.

I want *my* home.

I've pushed the amount of time a person can spend in a restaurant to the unconscionable limit.

I am so tired.

I think about the grass and trees of the courthouse.

I return to the Tourism Center and Museum. I find the shade of a tree, an area obscured from street view, not that there are many people on the street to worry about. I try to sleep with my backpack for a pillow, but it's too uncomfortable, and I am too keyed up anyway. But I feel relatively safe and okay here, it is quiet. Then I feel this little sting. I just got bit on my leg by something. And I notice these really nasty looking red ants scurrying in the underneath of the emerald turf, so I decide it's probably better not to sleep on the grass. I'll just sit here a spell and try to watch out.

I call my dad.

I tell him what has happened.

I tell him where I am. He tells me he knows Holbrook well, actually. He has done a lot of research on the Navajo reservation and Holbrook is the closest major town. (My dad is a sociologist.) He asks how long I have been homeless here.

I have been here now for over six hours.

I tell him, "I will never get these hours of my life back."

"I am sure Stephen King could write a good story about being stuck in Holbrook," my dad says.

"Yes, yes," I say. "Don't worry. I will write something about this place, but right now I'm too freaked out about everything."

Then he tells me how it could have been worse. This is my dad's version of optimism. All the time he tells people how it could be worse.

I don't call my mom because I know it will just make her worry like crazy. Worry is often her version of thinking, especially about people she loves. A crinkle wears between her eyes and her mouth turns down and sometimes she gets terrible migraines and breathes in gasps like she's forgotten to inhale for a couple of minutes. I don't want to do that to her, when she is finally with all my siblings and so happy to see everyone. She will say to me, after I have arrived, "I'm glad I didn't know you were stranded out there. I would have been so *worried.*"

All is Well

When my brother finally arrives, I feel such intense relief I nearly cry. He tells me, half-joking, that this was God's way of saying I should have ridden with him in the first place. I relay how horrible this experience has been for me, and how it had seemed so important that I go on my own. My sweet little niece, from her car seat in the back, offers me her special keychain, an "I Heart 66" that my brother bought for her on the road. She gives it to me to hold, so I will feel better.

We drive for a long while, but as it gets dark and it is raining bugs on the rural roads, he wants to stop for the night. I vote to keep going. I want to drive—God, I am aching to keep moving keep moving. All night, really. I can drive all night I tell him.

But I drive for about twenty minutes, into a small town called Springerville and get pulled over for speeding. I've never had a speeding ticket in my life.

This seems like the sign to call this day quits.

We stop in Springerville for the night.

We call my dad and all the rest of the family, who have already arrived at the reunion. I have been rescued and we, the last of the family still on the road, will be there tomorrow. As much as I had feared them thinking me irresponsible or suggesting I was dumb for having had such a stupid accident, I don't care anymore. I just want out of Arizona and I want family around me like a blanket. My family of hearty, take-care-of-business, musical, boisterous people. My ancestors who crossed the plains to Utah with handcarts. My ancestors who sang in the midst of life-threatening trouble the traditional hymn "Come, Come Ye Saints" for which the chorus is the refrain, "All is Well." My people.

All is well, I tell my family on the phone.

I am in the same bed as my niece. She quickly is asleep, twisted like a small letter *c*. I quietly move my mouth to the Kundalini protection chant. I wish I'd remembered it earlier. I would have been using it all day. Wish I had done it before I began my drive this morning. Maybe it would have saved me.

Aad guray nameh...
Jugaad guray nameh...
Sat guray nameh...
Siree guroo dayvay nameh...

I use my fingers like a rosary and do it five times. Twenty fingers.

I sleep and dream something I want to forget. So I do forget it. I don't remember it now.

New Mexico > Arizona

I cheer when we enter New Mexico. I like the little dumpy towns in New Mexico worlds above the ones in Arizona. I even like the names of the towns better: Magdalena, Truth or Consequences, or my favorite, a town of about forty people called House. I used to live in one of these dumpy little towns, when we moved here after the divorce. This state is, in most places, a flat land, drab, squalid and full of nothing. But I love its' own brand of nothing. I remember the first time my mom and I drove into New Mexico to find a house. I remember my sense of shock that I would be living here. It felt like another planet, back then. It is a home planet, now.

We stop in Magdalena at the one open gas station (it is July 4th) and there is a young woman working there who seems about 18 or 20. There are what I call "pin-up Jesus pics" all over the walls. You know the ones, where he is so dreamy and holding out his glowing heart 'cause it's for you, too. (I collect these sorts of pictures.)

Me, my brother and his kids, we are a talkative bunch, and the young woman is so kind and humble, like she is so glad we are there with all our noises and needs. Me, looking at the pickled peppers, glad they aren't pigs feet (not looking too closely either). All of us descending upon the restroom, the only people in this gas station save for this young woman. And I am taken with her. With her sweet face and who she is and knowing she is in this town for what will seem like forever, and she's okay with it.

And then we get back on the road where your cell phone won't work because there is no service—there is nothing, but just dry, flat land—and I start rhapsodizing to my brother about how that young woman in the gas station *really* loves Jesus, because it shines all over her. "It's real for her," I say. "It's not just that she has pictures on the wall, it's not something she says, it's how she *is* every day of her fucking life."

But I don't actually say the "fucking" part because there are kids in the car, and I don't swear around my family. A swear word is like a slap to them. I say "gosh" and "heck" and "crap" around my family. And "screw." As in, "I really screwed up my car."

Older

We arrive at the reunion in Ruidoso that afternoon. Our group is staying at a lodge, and we have taken over most of the place. All of my little nieces and nephews are playing on the lawn. I yell at them to come and hug me because that's part of the understood contract of having an aunt, and they huddle and carefully throw their little arms around me and each other. I am that weird aunt that they like, but they haven't quite figured out yet.

Some of my brothers and sisters and spouses are sitting comfortably on the porch, sedentary as if they hadn't moved from those positions all day.

"Oh, don't get up," I joke, because none of them do upon seeing me, giving me a casual greeting like I was just late getting up that morning. "No! Get up and hug me now!" I then demand of each of them, in turn.

I fill in the details about why we're late and the struggle to get here, but by this point it's old news and they seem far more interested in my dye job—stark white hair with purple streaks fading to light blue. My sister T. says it reminds her of cotton candy and she wants to take a bite out of my head. My brother C. says I look like Elsa from *Frozen*. My brother M. says, "Well, what's the deal with that? Is it for a part or something?" They are accustomed to the idea of me needing to do something crazy as an actor.

"No," I say. "I just felt like I've had the same hair my whole life, and I wanted to do something drastic to show that this is now. Everyone always thinks I am younger than I am, too. Something about white makes me feel like it's okay to age."

"It makes you look older," my dad agrees.

***

Ruidoso has magnificent natural landscape. This is one of the few towns in the state that is up in the mountains, with ski hills open during the winter. Pine trees and deer are everywhere, and everything feels comforting. It is nicer than I anticipated it would be, not only this town but being around my family.

The kids are a mess of all ages, but the years since I've last seen them have transformed them into different people entirely. The smaller ones band together around the pool table playing some sort of pre-school version of the game where they roll the balls across at each other and into the holes. Every once in a while they scream about how one of them is cheating.

The teenagers have clumped together in circles playing boardless, cardless games like Paranoia, Mafia and Werewolf. I loiter around the perimeter, and they invite me to join. I play one round of Paranoia and call it quits. "I am paranoid enough already," I say.

Though I am enjoying myself, I can't ignore the anxious feeling I have being without my car. I am fixed on an idea that everyone in my family needs to know that I can take care of myself, that I am not some flighty actor/writer/director/whatever but someone who can pay her bills and survive independently. But here and now, I am not self-sufficient. I am still stranded. For this week, I am beholden to others for rides, which of course, they are happy to give me. My dad even offers and rises early to take me to a yoga class because I tell him, "Yoga is my anti-depressant."

I still have the story to write. I have a deadline. And I must re-envision the whole thing, starting with the end. The narrator being repulsed and horrified at the sight of an old, bloody creature (now I see it eating a heart that is bloated with maggots) (now I see that the creature stares at her with one blue-green eye) only to realize that it is actually the narrator (oh God, that's me, that's me) in a mirror—

—nope.

I don't want it anymore. Now it is only home I want for an ending.

How do I write myself home?

But instead of writing anything, I spend every spare second on the phone with the mechanic in Holbrook working out the details of getting my car fixed, and with my insurance adjustor dealing with that bureaucratic nightmare. I also have to sign up for online traffic school to expunge the speeding ticket.

And I feel so exhausted by the time the sun sets.

And I realize it's not just my dye job.

I really *am* older.

A Message from the Future

One of the nights, my dad presents a digital album of old photos of all of us that he's scanned into his computer. He'd been compiling these pictures for months. My dad is a great photographer with a keen eye. There is one that captures two of my brothers in the foreground and my mother reflected in a mirror in the background—it is such a cinematic picture, a still you might see in a Kubrick movie. We watch this retrospective of our family, through all the years and bad fashion trends and absurd haircuts.

And then there is a picture of me and my cousin Heidi. None of my nieces and nephews know who she is, and my older sister R. says, "She is the one that died. She was hit by a car. It was a sixteen year old driver."

We are all haunted by this face. There is proof in that face of the indifference, or the injustice, of God. The random accident that takes the life of a child. She was my peer, my age, my friend. Her death so sudden—she was running across the street without a care in the world as most kids do and then, in an instant, her life was over.

"*Never* run across a street or a parking lot," I say the next day, yelling out to my little nieces and nephews after I observe them doing it. None of them listen to me. They nod and agree and then they do it once again right before my eyes. I don't even want to think about it, it makes my stomach hurt with worry.

I tell their mom, my younger sister R., an inspiring mother, that she needs to make sure her kids know better. She has told them, too, of course. But, I insist, she needs to make it stick. I tell my sister to have a "Come to Jesus" talk with them about it. I explain what a "Come to Jesus" talk means. I explain how important it is that her kids be more careful. And I hear myself going on about it, me without children who has just wrecked her own car and had to be rescued. Then, I take a deep breath.

"It's a wonder you all have survived so long without me around, telling you what to do all the time," I say.

After the slide show, it is evening, and the teenagers crowd into the hot tub at the lodge and tell scary stories. My niece A. calls me over. They all invite me in. I sit near the edge, though, not getting in. I listen to their stories about a mysterious girl in a red dress, a spooky house, a man with a hook, a man with a freaky smile, and some that are funny scary stories, like the one about the coffin that gets cured by a cough drop.

Then I tell them the scariest true story I know:

"I have a message from the future…your parents and I… we were once *you*. And one day, you will be *us*."

"Would You Rather Be Eaten By...?"

The last night of the reunion there is a talent show. I watch them all like a proud parent, the way they sing and play the piano, how my mom learned a ten page Bach piece just for this occasion. How my sister T. learned to play the lute two months prior, and plays sweetly, her hands shaking, apologizing because she is so nervous and insisting we have to just hear her play it on the porch tomorrow, she really does know it.

My two nieces L. and N.—both under the age of seven—put their arms around each other and sing "Let it Go." While perhaps cliché, I cry so hard watching them my body shakes and snot runs down my face. No one else is so moved, but something about it kills me, these gorgeous little girls with faces like my sister singing about how they are going to let themselves express who they are. Then at the end, my dad has put together a book of poetry for everyone, to encourage his grandchildren to learn to like it.

My dad asks me to come up and read a couple of verses from his compilation. I am surprised, but if he wants me to come up and flap my mouth, I was born ready. Before I begin reading, however, I tell the crowd that my two favorite poems are currently "In the Desert" by Stephen Crane and "Psalm of Life" by Longfellow. I once had each of them memorized but not anymore. Anyway, I quote what I remember. "*Life is real! Life is earnest! And the grave is not its goal,*" I tell them. "*...But I like it. Because it is bitter. And because it is my heart.*'" My brother C. calls out that I have a creepy picture on my website that shows me eating my own heart like in this poem. I tell them all, yes, there is a portrait of me done by the artist Jim Agpalza, that is an homage to this poem. I explain to them that in my picture, though, my heart is not bitter. It is a red velvet cupcake with frosting. It is a sweet heart. And mine to eat.

I tell them this portrait will be the cover of my newest book, a collection of my short stories. I tell them there is only one final story left to write, which I meant to accomplish here but now I will have to wait until I get home and I can screw my head on straight. I say, maybe some of the kids will be able to read this collection when they are older, and for some of the adults, they too might want to give it a try. It will not contain quite as much profanity as my novels do.

Then I read, per request, "The Ballad of the Harp Weaver" by Edna St. Vincent Millay.

After the talent show, some people stay up late eating Oreo shakes. I am trying to figure out how to make a s'more with all the ingredients but without a fire or microwave.

My older sister R., an artist and a warrior, asks me, in a voice like a Disney princess, "Would you rather be eaten by a mountain lion, a bear, or a shark?"

I think about it.

"A shark would be the least painful and fastest," she tells me.

But I choose a mountain lion because of my love of cats.

"I feel there would be something okay about my life being submitted to a Cat-Goddess," I say.

That makes her laugh. She says she would prefer a mountain lion as well, but for a different reason. She'd prefer it because it has the least scary face.

My New Tattoo

The next morning, before I leave the reunion, my niece A. agrees that I can draw on her hand with a ballpoint pen. I ask her what she wants me to draw, and she requests a spider.

"But a spider like a Spiderman spider," she says, which I

can't do. I draw a spider with a smiley face, and little shorts on all of its legs. Then I ask her to draw a spider on me, in return. She draws a spider that actually appears life-like.

When I see it in the mirror I feel stronger. I feel like it is protection.

It is early evening when my brother S., his kids and I finally pack up the car and drive away. We say our goodbyes, and I hug everyone I can, holding on for too long.

At our overnight stop at a motel to break up the trip, I add more ink to my spider with the pen in the room. I want to make the drawing last. The next morning, still in my brother's car, I find another pen to put even more ink. The ink is silver. It reminds me of a dream my friend recently told me about. A vivid dream that I was colored all black and white like a film noir, and I gave him a tattoo with weird silver ink under his skin and uttered the words, "Sacred Geometry."

This spider is *my* dream tattoo. I even say it aloud as I look at the silver spider on my hand: "Sacred Spider."

I want to keep it forever.

None of the Above

Something else. The evening we leave the reunion, we drive on serene rural roads and as dusk descends I see more deer than I have ever seen in my life. They bound from the road towards the wilderness as we approach.

Night falls, and I turn around to nag my niece and nephew into sharing a blanket with each other in the backseat.

And my brother S. swerves the wheel hard. The car shakes and quickly gains control.

I turn back to my brother. "Did you see it?!" he asks.

He had just missed hitting a mountain lion.

He is in awe.

"I don't really want to be eaten by a Cat-Goddess," I say

in a whisper. "I don't want to be eaten at all." Just to make sure that whoever is writing this story knows.

Whoever you are…I just want to go home.

The Sweat Lodge

The mechanic in Holbrook, who is north of eighty years, sees through watery blue eyes behind thick glasses and speaks with a slow, measured but loud twang. He runs through a few times everything they could not fix on my car, such as finding a part even after they tried to order it from Michigan.

So Ms. Thang still needs work. But she should get me to Flagstaff. Then I should check the wear on the tires. And maybe I'll have to find a mechanic there.

Or, maybe just maybe…

She can get me home.

But as I get her back on the road for the first time in a week, my shoulders tensed up near my ears, it's obvious my car is not quite right. Every sound she makes is different. I don't think of her as spectacular Ms. Thang at the moment, I think of her as elderly and messed up. My guilt for hurting her is now gone. Now, it's about survival. Will she get me home? Can she get me home *today*?

She endures up until Flagstaff, and there, I get out and see that part of the plastic underneath her front bumper is jetting out and twisted against the tires, so I muscle it back into shape and under the car.

My brother rides in tandem with me, though it means he has to drive much slower because my little car is struggling to keep up with him.

Just out of Flagstaff, my car's red temperature warning gauge comes on as we ascend a long, steady hill. To be fair to her, it is 115 degrees Fahrenheit outside. I pull over on the freeway. In front of me, my brother sees me and does the same. He approaches the car and tells me if the engine fully overheats we will need to abandon it. He is right. It is too hot and it's not safe to be on the freeway and not safe to be outside in this egregious heat.

With the car running, he steps inside, switches off my AC and blasts the heat.

The warning gauge goes off.

Keeping the heat running will minimize chances of overheating.

He gets back in his car, going even slower now. I drive with my hazards on, my windows down and the heat on full blast in the middle of a burning hell desert.

I get my sweat lodge.

It is my own car.

She's doing fine, now. We can keep going, I text my brother. Let's keep going. I get a heat rash on my legs where my heater is blasting. I pour water over my head. My face is bright red.

I watch in dismay, with my wet hands clutching the steering wheel, as my Sacred Spider, my tattoo from my niece A., disappears in the salt water of my flesh.

My mind is not quite right, I think. I am telling myself I need to really be honest now, about how okay in the head I am, because as bad as overheating in the desert may be, fainting behind the wheel of a moving car is how *it could be worse*.

My brother texts that we are going to stop at the next exit.

Oh, yes. Thank you.

We pull into a gas station, the only services for miles, littered with weary travelers, lots of flies, and a Dairy Queen. We are in California at last, and I am in love with every weirdo I see. I don't want food, but I sure want ice cream.

My brother treats me to a vanilla twist soft-serve that towers over its cone.

I say, “I want to dump this right on my head!” to my niece and nephew, and they laugh. But I don’t do it. Instead, we all eat it.

The Mirage

I keep going. I get to the part where the 58 freeway splits from the 15, and my brother goes his way to Bakersfield and I go mine to L.A. It’s okay, now. My car is doing okay like this, and the air is cooling down a bit. I am no longer blasting the heat, but I play it cautious and endure with no AC, going slow on hills. I continue making progress.

As I near Los Angeles, I am in love with the traffic, with the vastness of the thousands of houses and buildings and billboards, with the trees that can only live from water stolen from non-desert areas but oh how I love these jewels of our thievery. I love all the lights and all of this illusion. I even love this smog. I love all these cars behind me that need to be somewhere right now, cars I am impeding by going the speed limit. I sing in an operatic style the city name Rancho Cucamonga as it approaches and long after I pass it. I catch myself in the mirror: white hair, red face, sunglasses.

See there, you in the mirror? You are not a naked bloated thing, bleeding out in the desert, heart in your hands. You are going to make it. Can you feel it?

The sun starts to set. It is cooling down, yes. I am soaked wet with sweat, bright red from the heat, and I stink, dear God do I stink, but my head is clear.

I will make it home.

I hope this is what it feels like to die. That is how happy I am. My heart feels out of my chest with all of the unbearable sweetness. This red velvet heart of mine. All mine.

Home stays just ahead of me. It shimmers. As I move, it moves too. It doesn't stay put. It is still in the distance *out there*.

Maybe it isn't even there at all.

But I am going to make it, all the same.

I just have to keep moving.

Acknowledgments

First, my sweetheart, Ezra Werb, who found and *took care of* countless nasty typos, unintentional nonsensical sentences, and read and read aloud these stories and helped most significantly in making my way through "In the Desert." My parents and my siblings, and all my nieces and nephews who inspire me, humble me, keep me honest, but most of all who love me no matter what. And then my *other* family, my Bizarro tribe. You make this planet a home planet. Rose O'Keefe, CEO of Eraserhead Press, who inspires us all with her huge can of whup-ass and who is one of the kindest, smartest and best all around humans. Jim Agpalza for the cover and for all of his amazing artistry.

The origin stories of *Angel Meat*:

"Happy Hour" first appeared in the anthology *Demons* and "The Liar" in *Psychos, Serial Killers, Depraved Madmen and the Criminally Insane*, both edited by John Skipp and published by Black Dog and Leventhal.

"Blue Velvet Cake" saw first light within the pages of *In Heaven, Everything is Fine* edited by Cameron Piece, published by Eraserhead Press.

"Lost Dog" was first found in *Explosions*, an anthology edited by Scott Bradley for MAG (the Mine Advisory Group).

"Tangerine," I wrote for my friend Katie Grant at her request for me to write her "a cheese doodle" for inspiration when she was going through chemo. It is included here as a tribute to her and her friendship.

"Blackout in Upper MooseJaw" was first seen in *Slave Stories: Scenes from the Slave State,* edited by Chris Kelso and published by Omnium Gathering.

"Rat-Head" in *Rough Magick* edited by Francesca Lia Block and Jessa Marie Mendez, dangerous angel.

"The Cause" in *You, Human* edited by Michael Bailey, Dark Regions Press.

All of the editors have my huge thanks for reaching out for a story. There would be no *Angel Meat* without these first 'asks'.

And finally, John Skipp. The list of specific thanks would be a book unto itself, but I will just say that he fights the good fight with and for all of us artists, a visionary who is our 'pal in the trenches.' He is one of my dearest friends in a way that is more like dearest family. Thank you for wanting this collection, thank you for being woven out of the same blanket, but most of all, thank you for helping me find my way home.

Laura Lee Bahr is a multi-award winning writer, performer and director. She is the author of *Haunt*, (Fungasm Press, winner of the Wonderland Book Award), which was translated into Spanish under the title *Fantasma* (Orciny Press, which was nominated for 'best translated novel', by the Kelvin 505 and the Ignotus awards) and *Long-Form Religious Porn* (Fungasm Press). Laura also has been a screenwriter for various award-winning films. Her debut feature as writer/director, *Boned*, won "Best Micro-Budget Feature" at the Toronto Independent Film Festival and is currently distributed through Gravitas (available everywhere). She lives in Los Angeles with her sweetheart and a couple of cats, still living the dream, she supposes.

You can follow her on social media and at
www.lauraleebahr.com

CPSIA information can be obtained
at www.ICGtesting.com
Printed in the USA
FSOW01n0201100517

9 781621 052258